MOLE IN THE MILITARY

For Maxin

I hope you enjoy the book

Mike Leeds

MOLE IN THE MILITARY

Mike Leeds

Book Guild Publishing
Sussex, England

First published in Great Britain in 2011 by
The Book Guild Ltd
Pavilion View
19 New Road
Brighton, BN1 1UF

Typesetting in Baskerville by
Nat-Type, Cheshire

Printed in Great Britain by
CPI Antony Rowe

A catalogue record for this book is available from
The British Library.

ISBN 978 1 84624 592 3

Chapter 1

It was about two o'clock on a sunny day in September. Sergeant James MacDonald pulled into the car park of a cemetery in Kent to attend the funeral at two-thirty of Captain 'Stony' Burke of 22 SAS and his twelve-year-old daughter, Nikki.

James got out of the car, took out a packet of cigarettes from his dark-grey suit, lit a cigarette and stood leaning against the car waiting for the funeral procession to arrive.

Major Tompsett had told James before he left Hereford that Captain Burke had been killed in a road traffic accident while driving with his daughter on a country road near their home. It had been a head-on collision with a lorry and the car had ended up a mangled heap; the lorry had driven away without stopping. 'I also want you to call in at Maidstone police station,' the Major told him, 'and see an Inspector Terry Reeves. See what you can find out about the accident.'

At last the funeral procession had arrived and Jill, Stony's wife, got out of the car. She was dressed in a black jacket and skirt with a white blouse underneath. She was pale and her eyes were red from crying, but she was still a beautiful woman. Jill grabbed hold of her son's hand as they waited for the coffins to be taken into the church then they followed them in. James sat at the back.

As the service proceeded James didn't pay much attention for he was thinking about Stony. He owed this man big time, he owed him his life, the biggest debt you could ever owe someone. It all happened in Bosnia when, as part of a four-

1

man brick, they had been on a reconnaissance patrol behind enemy lines. They were just going to cross a road and then it all went wrong. A group of Serbian soldiers opened fire with AK-47s and a bullet hit James in the upper thigh in the right leg, the bullet clipping the bone on the way through, James screamed, grabbing his wounded leg as he stumbled and fell in the road. Stony, though, turned back and ran to James while Sergeants 'Ginger' White and Ian 'Willie' Nelson covered him.

Stony grabbed hold of James and lifted him to his feet, and half running and half being dragged, James made it into the woods on the other side of the road.

James' face was as white as a sheet. 'I can't make it go, get out of here.'

'Come on, move, Sergeant! That's an order. Let's go! Go, go!'

Stony grabbed hold of James, who cried out in pain.

'Come on, take the pain! We've got to get deeper into the wood. Then we'll worry about that wound.'

'Bastard!' James said through clenched teeth.

Bullets were whistling through the trees. Ginger and Willie were still firing from the edge of the wood keeping the Serbs' heads down as the four comrades made it deeper into the wood. They stopped in an area where the undergrowth was thicker, giving them more cover to see to James.

Stony made James comfortable and reached for the field dressing connected to the webbing.

The exit wound was bigger than the entrance hole so Stony used a Tampax to plug the exit hole, covered it with lint and tied it securely into position with the bandage. Another field dressing was placed over the top.

The blood had stopped seeping through bandage but James was not in any condition to go on.

James looked at Stony. 'You've to go, you'll not make it with me in tow. You won't have the firepower to deal with them. It will be swarming with troops shortly.'

Stony knew James was right and found a hiding place in the undergrowth, made him as comfortable as he could, and then they took off. 'We'll be back, I promise,' Stony said.

Then they were gone. Now he was on his own. He looked at his watch. Twenty past ten. He checked his weapons. The pain was getting more intense and he was swearing at himself not to give in, take the pain and to survive.

It was night-time and the wood was damp. He was feeling cold. All he wanted to do was sleep but that would be suicidal. To keep awake, he forced himself to remember how his mates had got their nicknames. Johnny ('Kiwi') Cooper got his because he was a New Zealander from Wellington – bloody obvious, that one; Captain 'Stony' Burke was named after the detective in *Hawaii Five-O*. 'Willie' Nelson got his from country and western singer, while White had red hair so it was obvious that his nickname would be 'Ginger'.

What the hell's that? James heard a noise which he recognized as a twig breaking under the pressure of someone's foot. They were coming his way. He reckoned they were about 70 metres away. He could even hear them talking to each other. The hairs stood up on the back of his neck. He tried to work out how many of them there were. From the noise and movement he would have said at least ten. There was no way he could outrun them so if he was spotted he would have to fight.

James reached down the outside of his combat trousers, pulled the Velcro apart and grabbed hold of the knife he had strapped to his lower leg. He repeated the same operation on the other leg. James remembered the look on the face of the Army tailor in Hereford when he walked into the shop with two pairs of suit trousers and two pairs of combat trousers and a knife.

'What can I do for you, Sir?' the tailor asked.

James had explained that he wanted a slit cut in the seam on the outside of each leg so he could remove the knife from the scabbard without having to pull the trouser leg up first.

'Can I've a look at that knife, please?' the tailor asked.

'Be my guest,' James replied.

The tailor pulled the knife from its scabbard and admired it. It sure was a beauty. The blade was about six inches long and the cutting edge was like a razor.

By now the Serbs were very close. James lay as still as possible; only his eyes were moving. He could hear his heart beating faster and he wondered if they could hear it.

One Serb stopped about ten feet away and leant his AK-47 against the tree. He spoke to one of his comrades and he moved off, leaving the soldier there fiddling in his breast pocket. He pulled out a packet of cigarettes and then a lighter. The flame flickered. James closed one eye so the glare from the flame didn't spoil his night vision. At that moment the Serb spotted him and made a grab for the AK-47 but didn't make it, for the next second a knife had found its target and was protruding out from his throat. The Serb slumped back against the tree and slid into a sitting position. The only sound was a gurgling sound as air from the windpipe mixed with the blood.

James inched his way forward until he reached the body and felt for a pulse. When he didn't find one he pulled the knife out and wiped the blood off on the Serb's jacket. 'You should have read the packet: smoking kills!' he whispered.

With help from the tree James managed to stand up but felt a bit light-headed. The wound had started to bleed again and the leg was throbbing like hell. *And that's where I'll be if I don't move!* Too late. There was a rustling noise. By the noise there was only one of them.

Keeping the tree trunk between him and the Serb, he watched as the soldier got level and could see his mate's legs. James didn't understand what he shouted but his knife was already out and, with his left hand clamped over the Serb's mouth and chin, he plunged the knife deep into the side of his neck, severing the jugular vein and nerves. He held on until the body slumped forward. It was a messy killing; he was covered in blood. He pulled the knife out, cleaned it on his victim and put it away again.

Exhaustion had taken its toll and James crawled back into cover. He was fighting to keep conscious and to focus on the job in hand and stay alive. Were his eyes playing tricks? He could see more movement down the track, then a Serb soldier came into view. He clicked the safety catch off and aimed. *Wait! Hold fire!* He waited as more soldiers came into sight. then fired a short burst of well-aimed shots. Two fell down straight away; the others dived for cover then returned fire. Bullets were hitting trees and whistling through the undergrowth, some were too close for comfort. He knew he was doomed. This was it. He would be overrun, but he would take as many of them with him as he could!

He whipped the magazine off, replaced it with a full one, then fired a short burst at the Serb position. More by luck than judgement a bullet had found its target: one of the Serbs was screaming in agony.

The ground seamed to vibrate as three explosions shook the night. *Fuck me!* James thought. *They're using hand grenades!* Then he realized that it was the Serb positions that were being attacked. Small arms fire rained down, cutting the rest of the Serbs to pieces. Then it all stopped as quickly as it had started.

James looked skywards. A religious man he was not but he said a big thank you nonetheless. Stony and the boys were back.

Stony crept towards James on his belly, calling out softly.

James called out, 'The cavalry arrived just in time.'

'Hold your fire! We're coming in!' Stony called.

He crawled over to James with a broad grin on his face. 'Looks as if The Shadow has struck again,' he said jokingly. James just grunted.

5

'Ginger, bring over your field dressing, his leg is leaking like a sieve!'

Ginger came over and passed Stony his field dressing. 'When we get back it's your turn to pay for the drinks but till then you'll have to make do with water.'

Ginger took out his canteen of water, cradled James' head and put the canteen to his lips so he could have a drink.

'Thanks,' James whispered.

'You stay alive, boy; I want my pint.' Ginger was the oldest of the group, so it didn't matter how old anybody was he would always call them 'boy'.

As Stony started to work on James, he instructed Ginger to get on the radio and get the chopper out.

'Hello foxtrot one four, this is delta two zero.'

'Hello this is foxtrot one four, coming in loud and clear.'

'Map reference for extraction 437684, I say again 437684,'

'Yes map reference 437684 OK.'

'OK, can you give me an ETA?' James heard Ginger saying through a blur.

'Forty minutes. Contact again when you hear the chopper. Out.'

'Forty minutes, Stony.'

'Right, let's get ready to move out. Ginger, you can take the first stint carrying James. We'll change over every 150 metres. I've tied his wrists together so they can be looped over your neck so he won't fall backwards.'

Willie gave a laugh.

'That will be two pints he'll want now, James.'

Stony and Willie lifted James on to Ginger's back.

'Let's go.'

Stony led off, Ginger followed and Willie was playing the role of tail-end Charlie which was to cover their backs. It was slow, cumbersome work.

At last they reached the edge of the wood and there was the road where all the trouble had started. They dropped down at the edge of the wood and scanned the hedgerow on the other side of the road for a gap. The field on the other side was the extraction zone. They were looking for any enemy troops also a gap or a place they could get on to the field quickly without wasting too much time, Willie spotted a gap in the hedgerow about thirty metres down the road. He pointed it out to the others. The only problem was that a fence with three strands of wire had been constructed to keep animals in; it wasn't ideal but it would have to do. Very slowly and quietly, keeping just inside the treeline, they made their way to where they were going to cross. They stopped and looked up and down the road. Nothing moved. There was no one in sight. They formed up in line abreast. One last look and listen. All quiet...

'Ready to go,' said Stony.

'Ready!' came the reply.

'Go!'

They set off at a quick walking pace and reached the fence on the other side of the road. Willie placed a foot on the bottom wire and pulled the next wire up and forced them apart as much as he could. Stony climbed though, then Ginger passed James through and then climbed through himself. He grabbed the wires so Willie could get through.

Once in the field Stony looked to see what cover there was. About forty metres in there was a small area with about half a dozen trees and a few bushes. Again it wasn't ideal but it would have to do. Stony had James on his back and gave the hand signal to move out. Willie and Ginger moved out to either side, leaving about a five-metre gap between them. All of them were sweating profusely from the exertion of the last thirty minutes. This was the time when it was so easy to lose the plot. They had to keep it all together and stay focused. When they reached their objective they moved into cover, placed James on the ground and had a drink of water. They gave some to James just to keep his mouth moist.

'We've made the extraction zone,' panted Willie. 'Now the difficult bit – the extraction.'

Willie was right. This was the most dangerous part because not only are you in an exposed area, but you've the noise of the helicopter coming into your position. The helicopter, too, was at its most vulnerable.

About twenty minutes latter, faintly they could hear the engine and rotor blades of the helicopter. Ginger grabbed the radio.

'Hello, foxtrot one four, this is delta two zero. Come in, please.'

'Hello, this is foxtrot one four. We're about half a mile from extraction point.'

'We're forty metres in from the north end of the field. Do you want to come in under smoke?'

Ginger told Stony what the pilot wanted. They each took a smoke grenade off their webbing, ran into the field, pulled the pins and threw them so as to form a rough triangle. They then ran back to where they had left James. The helicopter engine and rotor were really throbbing on the radio.

'Delta two zero, this is foxtrot one four; I see smoke. I'm coming in straight and low. Be ready! I don't want to be on the ground long.'

'Roger to that. Out.'

They grabbed James and ran towards the smoke. Then all hell broke loose. Small arms fire was fired at the helicopter and the two machine gunners on board returned the fire with devastating effect. The pilot landed bang in the middle of the smoke. One of the machine gunners helped lift James on board and the others jumped in. The pilot opened the throttle and the helicopter lifted off the ground and gained height, the machine gunners still spraying the Serb positions with instant death. Once they were out of range Stony turned to the gunner and shouted.

'Where's the rock n' roll music I've seen on the films when the helicopter comes in?'

'You've seen too many war films. This is the real world.'

As soon as they landed at base, a meat wagon rushed over, loaded James on board, then drove away at high speed. It was touch and go. James spent three weeks in hospital and nine weeks in a rehabilitation unit.

Chapter 2

The service had finished and the congregation filed out of the church to the cemetery, first the two coffins, then Jill, her son and an elderly man with silver hair. Jill was holding his arm. It could be her or Stony's father. The rest of the mourners followed, James brought up the rear. At the graveside, James stayed a little bit away but could see all that was going on. Jill and her son, Ben, had two red roses in their hands. The vicar moved to the head of the grave and said a few words about Stony's life, only he called him Roy. Half of what he was saying James didn't recognize. The vicar said that Roy was a devoted husband to Jill and father to Nikki and Ben, also that he was a serving officer in the 22 SAS. Nikki, he said, had been a very bright, loveable child who was a credit to her parents and had had many friends at school and her ambition had been to go to university to study law. All this was true but, to James, Stony had been a man's man, hard as nails, one of the only Ruperts he would follow through hell and back.

As the coffins were lowered slowly into the grave, Jill and Ben threw their roses after the coffins. Jill pulled Ben to her and gave him a mother's hug.

The vicar picked up a handful of earth and threw it on top of the coffins, 'Ashes to ashes, dust to dust...' He turned to Jill, held her hands and had a word with her.

Jill then saw James and walked across to him and put her arms out. He grabbed her and held her tight for a while. With tears in her eyes she said, 'James, thank you for coming. It is good to see you. I know Roy meant a lot to you.'

'He meant the world to me, more than you'll ever know. I owe him such a lot.'

Still holding James tight, she asked, 'Will you come to the house? We've laid on food and drinks.'

'No,' James said, 'But I would like to come around tomorrow and maybe I could pick you up and we could go out to lunch and afterwards come back here and see the flowers on the grave. I would love to come back but today you should just be with your family.'

Jill kissed him and as she walked away she said, 'See you tomorrow.'

James returned to his car and sat there smoking a cigarette, waiting for all the mourners to leave to go to Jill's house. Once they had all left James drove out of the car park and went to a motel he had seen on his way to the funeral. He went into reception and booked a room for two nights because he had an appointment at Maidstone police station the day after tomorrow.

James got his case out of the boot of his car and took it up to his room. It was pretty basic but comfortable enough. He took off his suit and, ever the soldier, put it neatly on a hanger and placed it in the wardrobe. He went into the bathroom and had a shower, returned to the bedroom, put on a clean pair of boxers and lay down on the bed. Soon he was fast asleep.

The next morning James pulled into Stony and Jill's crescent-shaped driveway. The house was old and outside the front door was a porch with a rose bush each side that had been trained to meet at the pitch of the roof. It was an idyllic place.

James knocked on the door and was greeted by Jill who asked him in. He followed her into the living room, where a fire blazed in the inglenook fireplace. Sitting on the settee was the gentleman who had been at the funeral and Jill was holding his arm.

'James, this is Albert, my father. Dad, this is James, a very good friend of Stony's.'

Her dad stood up and shook hands. 'I've heard all about you. Jill was telling me last night.'

'I hope it was all good,' James replied.

'Nothing to worry about, son.'

'Dad is going to look after Ben for me.'

'That's good of him.'

'I still have my use.'

'I bet you do. By the way, where is the little fellow?'

'He's upstairs in his room reading a book. He spends a lot of time on his own. I think it will take a while before he adjusts, but children seem to adjust better than adults.'

'That's true,' said James.

James fumbled in his pocket and pulled out an envelope and passed it to Jill. She opened the envelope and pulled out a card signed by all his comrades. Inside the card was a cheque for two thousand pounds. Jill's eyes filled with tears.

'Look, Dad.' She showed him the cheque.

'What a pleasant surprise. What will you do with it?'

'I'll get a headstone for Roy's grave. What do you think?'

'Good idea, love.'

'When one of our own gets killed we hold an auction for his kit, so you can see how much Stony meant to his mates.'

'Stony? Where did that come from?' Albert asked.

James explained and Jill's dad laughed. 'Have you all got nicknames?'

'Most of us,' James replied.

'Have *you* got one?' Albert asked.

'Yes but if I tell you I'd have to kill you.' They were all laughing.

Jill piped up. 'He's called The Shadow because he moves like one.'

'Stony's been talking again.'

'I'll just pop upstairs and put my face on and see Ben

12

before we go.' Jill went upstairs and when she had left James turned to Albert.

'How is she coping?'

'She'll manage! She's stronger than you think, but it has hit her hard.'

'Life still goes on.'

'I didn't want her to marry Roy. Not because I didn't like him, mind; it was because of the job.'

'I can understand that. I was married but she couldn't take the pressure. She didn't know when I would be called away or where I was going or if I was coming back in one piece. She gave me an ultimatum – the job or her. I told her I was a soldier and knew nothing else.'

Jill came down the stairs. She looked a picture. She was wearing a black dress that hugged her figure and finished just above her knee.

'Thanks, Dad.' She kissed him on the cheek. 'Are you ready, James?'

'When you are.' James turned to Albert shook his hand. 'I hope we meet again sometime.'

'So do I.'

A few minutes later James parked the car at the cemetery. The grave had been filled in and the flowers and wreaths were laid out on the earth, James held Jill's hand as they walked to the grave. She bent down and turned the labels so she could read them to see whom they were from. The flowers were beautiful. There was a big cross made from white flowers with the name 'Roy' written in red roses and a smaller one to match with 'Nikki' on it. After about forty minutes they returned to the car.

In The White Hart Inn, where he had booked a table in the small, cosy restaurant, James wondered how he could broach the difficult subject. He decided it was best to be direct.

'Jill, can I ask you a couple of questions? I'm sorry but Major Tompsett has told me to go to see Chief Inspector Terry Reeves about the accident.'

'I know but I don't understand why.'

'It's military procedure. They want a report on file about what happened. It's hard for me as well.'

'I know. Go ahead – ask away.'

'On the morning of the accident where did Stony go?'

'He went to play golf at the local golf club with his dad. That's why Nikki went with him – to see her granddad.' Tears welled in her eyes.

'I'm sorry, just one more. Did you get any telephone calls that morning. Think carefully.'

'My father phoned to ask us to go around to him for dinner on Saturday.'

'Any more? Think hard.' James topped up the wine glasses and then looked at Jill intently.

'There *was* one more call. I answered it. Roy had already left.'

'Who was it?'

'He said he was a mate of Roy's. I told him I could take a message for him, but he said he would call back later.'

'Any more?'

'No, that was it.'

'Good, let's enjoy our lunch.' He gave her a smile, even though he was hurting inside.

After the meal they sat there finishing the wine. Jill picked up her handbag and pulled out a small box.

'James, I want you to have this.' She passed the box across the table to him.

James opened it. It was a watch, an expensive one.

'I can't accept it, Jill. It should go to Ben or one of the family.'

'Please, James, he would want you to have it. He never wore it to work; that's why I still have it. *Please* take it.'

James wiped a tear from his eye. He reached over and held her hand, looking into her eyes. 'Thank you.'

On the way back to Jill's house they were mostly silent, each lost in their own thoughts. But as Jill got out of the car he said:

'You know what my job is and I'm away a lot but can I give you a ring and have a meal together again?'

'I would like that, James. I've enjoyed today.'

'Fantastic.'

She kissed him on the cheek and he waved to her as she walked up to the house and went inside.

Chapter 3

At Maidstone police station the desk sergeant was standing behind the desk talking to a lady in her sixties. The sergeant's hair had receded and he had more head to polish than hair to cut and what hair that was left was more grey than black. He was overweight but from the way he carried his frame he was probably a fit athletic man about ten years ago. The lady was in her sixties and was large, with big boobs and a big backside. She wore glasses with thick tortoiseshell frames and was dressed in a grey checked jacket and skirt. She reminded James of Miss Marple. She was complaining that she was being stalked by a good-looking man in his early thirties, white with brown hair cut short. James smiled to himself. You should be so lucky.

While the sergeant took down her statement, James looked at the posters on the walls, mostly missing persons. One of them sent a shiver down his spine. It was a young girl about Nikki's age and had an uncanny resemblance to her.

Miss Marple was still ranting. The man, it seemed, had made improper suggestions to her.

'Like what?' asked the Sergeant.

Her face went red as she answered, 'You don't get many of those to the pound. I'd love to play with those melons!'

James turned his face away, trying to stop himself from laughing. He looked at the clock on the wall behind the counter. Twelve minutes before his appointment. At last Miss Marple finished and turned to walk out of the door. She

16

turned back again. 'You'll let me know the result of your investigation, Sergeant?'

'Yes I will,' the sergeant replied.

When she had left James got up and walked over to the counter.

'Was that for real?'

'Yes, she comes in about every six weeks with the same story but the description of the man changes. We find the best way to deal with it is to humour her; otherwise she phones the Inspector. What can I do for you, Sir?'

'Sergeant James MacDonald. I've an appointment with Chief Inspector Terry Reeves,' James replied.

'Can you just wait for a minute, I'll ring through to see if he's free.' He picked up the telephone and tried the Inspector's extension number. It rang for only about three seconds.

'Sir, I've a Sergeant James MacDonald to see you.'

He replaced the receiver. 'I'll get someone to take you to his office.'

James followed a young officer along a corridor with photographs on the walls of the police football team spaced at about six feet apart with the year and position they finished in the league on a plaque over the top. They climbed two flights of stairs and went along another corridor; this time the photographs were of the police shooting teams. At the end of the corridor they stopped at a door with a brass plate with the words 'Chief Inspector' engraved on it. Cheapskates! James thought, they didn't even have his name on it.

The Chief Inspector was a smallish man in his fifties, a little too small, James thought, to have joined the force without some string-pulling. He was of slim build with weasel features and a big scar that ran from his eye to the corner of his mouth. He was smartly dressed and could clearly command respect just by his presence.

'I'm grateful for you seeing me, Sir. Major Tompsett asked me to come to see you and then report back to him. I should stress I'm not here to step on your toes, Sir, or in any way get involved in investigating this accident; I've just come to see what information you can give me.'

'I appreciate that, Sergeant. the frank and honest approach. Often when we deal with the military they tend to try to take over.'

'When one of our own is involved, Major Tompsett always tries to get the facts on file. But he says it's a civil matter, not one to interfere in.'

'Would you like a tea or coffee?'

'Black coffee no sugar, please.'

While they were waiting for the coffee, the two men made small talk.

'I really liked the photographs of the shooting teams. Have you got a range on site?'

'No we use the local range. One hundred metres is the longest range we have, but for full bore we hire Hythe Ranges.'

'Well, how about if I ask Major Tompsett if we could arrange a shooting match with your team. It wouldn't cost the police a penny.'

'Brilliant.'

'I'll get the Major to contact you and we'll even lay on the refreshments.'

'Sounds great.'

There was a knock on the door and in came the young officer with a tray. The Chief Inspector grabbed a file off his desk, opened it, and they got started.

'I'll tell you what we have to date, then you can ask any questions afterwards. Is that all right?'

'Fine, Sir.'

'The accident happened on 15 September at approximately 1300 hours. The lorry driver, it seems, left the scene before the police arrived, but left the lorry where it was. Mr Burke and his daughter, Nikki, were pronounced dead at the scene. The lorry was stolen from a company based in Bow, East London, owned by J.D. Hall and Sons. They say that the lorries are parked up overnight in their compound after being refuelled except if they're out working. This one was parked in the yard, so it didn't have to be filled up at all.

'The driver of the lorry knew what he was about – he wiped all fingerprints from the steering wheel and door handles – so clearly we're dealing with a known criminal. We've no idea what the lorry was going to be used for: it could be a ram raid on cash machines or just to carry stolen property. Mr Burke and his daughter didn't stand a ghost of a chance, though … That's about all we 'ave.'

James nodded his head and asked, 'Do you still have the vehicles here. I'd like to have a look at them.'

'Yes, they're in the compound at the rear of the building, I'll arrange for an officer to show you.'

'Thank you, Sir,' James replied. 'I'd also like to see where the accident happened, if possible. Could you show me on the map?'

'I'll do better than that: I'll get the officer to show you after he has taken you to see the vehicles. Have you got a car with you?'

'Yes, Sir, in the car park.'

'Well, you can follow him to the scene of the accident.'

'Thank you, Sir. I really do appreciate your cooperation and hospitality.'

The Inspector picked up the telephone and dialled an extension number. 'Constable Holder, can you come to my office. I've a job for you.'

'Thanks again, Sir.'

'No bother. Just remember to arrange the shoot and I'll hopefully see you again.'

Constable Mark Holder knocked on the door and was called in.

Once outside the office, James turned to the young officer. 'No need to call me, Sir. My name's James. May I call you Mark?'

'Please do,' Mark said with a big grin on his face. At last someone was treating him like an equal, not like a kid.

The vehicle compound at the rear of the police station was surrounded by a galvanized palisade fence three metres high.

'This way, James, the lorry and the car are parked over on the far side.'

James walked over to the grey Ford Escort. It looked like a convertible because the roof had been cut off to get the bodies out. The front was crushed like a tin can and every window was smashed.

Mark was following him around the car like a puppy dog. 'They didn't stand a chance, did they?'

'Not a chance.'

'Look at all the blood over the seats, even in the back.'

'It's the force of impact,' James replied. 'Now would you like to help me?'

Marks eyes lit up. 'What can I do?'

'If you go around to the near side and look under the wheel arches and see if there is a small magnetic box, just big enough to hold a spare key and a ID card. Also, check the tyres for cuts and take a sample of the mud.'

'I can do that.'

Mark moved round to the near side of the car. James waited until he had bent down and his head was out of sight, and then reached into the car and felt under the dashboard. There it was! He pulled out the 9-mm Walther PPK in its holster and slipped it quickly into his jacket pocket. He wasn't really interested in the lorry. He had got what he wanted and he knew he wouldn't learn any more. He would have to keep up the pretence, though, so if the Chief Inspector questioned Mark he would only tell him what he saw. He knew the pistol was loaded because it was pointless carrying an empty weapon. He was just glad that it hadn't been found because the police didn't like guns on the streets.

'There's nothing here. Could it be anywhere else?' Mark asked as he reappeared.

'No, it was only the ID card I was interested in really.'

James had another look around. 'Let's check the lorry.'

After about twenty minutes James called it a day. Mark showed him the way to his car and said, 'I'll go and pick up the patrol car then you can follow me to the crash site.'

'OK, thanks.'

James got into his car feeling very pleased with himself. He had an extra weapon – no numbers, untraceable.

Mark pulled up alongside and raised his thumb in the air. James reciprocated and off they went. It was like a Sunday ride out into the country. The road twisted its way across open pastureland and was just fenced either side of road with strands of wire nailed to chestnut posts. Then the road made a real sharp bend to the left and immediately started to climb up a long steep hill with banks about three metres high on either side. Three-quarters of the way up the hill, Mark slowed down and flashed his lights, opened his window and pointed to the bank. There were tyre marks as if a car had tried to drive up the bank. Mark continued up the hill about a third of a mile and pulled into a lay-by.

James pulled in behind the police car, got out and walked over to the passenger side and got in beside Mark.

'I'm sorry but this is the closest we can park, but did you see the tyre marks in the bank? The lorry bloody nigh pushed him over the top.'

'It's fine, I can walk from here. When you get back, can you thank the Inspector? And thank *you*, too, Mark. You've been a great help.'

21

'It's been a pleasure, James. You've let me help and not left me to stand about like a spare prick at a wedding.'

'Well, you're right about that – you'll never learn by standing around.'

James shook his hand then walked back to his car and locked it. He waited until the patrol car was out of sight then walked up the hill away from the crash site. When he got to the top of the hill there was a gate on the left leading into a large field. James climbed the gate. To the left the ground fell away sharply and you could see across the low land where the road which they had driven along snaked through the fields.

James searched the area inside the gate. There were no signs of tracks; the rain had seen to that. James' eyes scanned the field higher up. There was a large knoll covered with bushes. He walked over to the foot of the knoll and began to search the ground. An hour later he found what he was looking for. One of the bushes had been cut and the earth cleared in such as away as to allow one person to crawl inside. The twigs that had been cut had been tied together with pieces of grass that had been plaited to make it stronger, forming a kind of camouflage hatch.

James crawled inside the bush. Tied to the camouflage 'hatch' was a piece of green cord that blended in with the foliage. He pulled the cord and fitted the 'hatch' back in place behind him. He was out of sight, but as he peered through the bush he saw that he had a clear view of the road below. The ground inside the hide was clear, except the occupant had overlooked a cigar butt. James took out his cigarette packet and put the butt inside.

Back in his car he rang Maidstone police station.

'Hello, Maidstone Police.' It was the same desk sergeant who replied.

'Can I speak to Chief Inspector Reeves. please?'

'Can I asked who is speaking?'

'Yes sorry, it's Sergeant MacDonald.'

'I'll try to put you through.' There was a pause.

'Hello, Sergeant Inspector Reeves. How can I help you?'

'I was wondering, Sir, whether your file on the accident includes the estimated speed of the car and lorry?'

'Hang on a minute, I'll have a look.' The phone went quiet and James heard the chair scrape across the floor and the rattle of a filing cabinet as it was opened.

'Ah here it is. I'm sorry I overlooked it. The car was doing about thirty miles an hour and the lorry seventy. He must have been driving like a lunatic.'

'Any idea why?' James asked.

'According to the file the officer attending the accident reckoned that he was running late so he had his foot to the floor.'

'Thank you, Sir, that's all I need to know. Goodbye.'

'Goodbye.' James tossed the phone on to the passenger seat.

Running late my arse! This was going to be the part where he shit himself or finished up in the local cemetery alongside Stony. He started the car and pushed his foot to the floor. His speed increased quickly; the needle was just over seventy and he was fighting to keep the car on the road. As soon as he was at the crash site he slowed down and looked at his watch; it had taken him four and a half minutes to reach the crash site. Now he would travel at thirty miles an hour for four and a half minutes and then see where he was. At four and a half minutes he was about twenty metres from a bridge that crossed over a stream. James pulled up on the bridge and looked to the right. He could see the knoll. This was the trigger point. As soon as Stony's car had come over the bridge the man at the observation point would have given a signal and sent the lorry on its way. This could have been by radio or mobile phone.

What the devil were you working on, Stony? This has all the hallmarks of an assassination.

23

James guessed there were four men involved: one watching Stony's house, the lorry driver, one in the observation post on the knoll and another to pick him up. It could be an active IRA cell, either sent from London or sent over from Ireland.

On the way back to the motel James pulled into a lay-by with a snack bar and ordered a black coffee and a bacon sandwich. He sat in his car thinking about the events of the day. Why hadn't the police picked up on the clues? They were there for all to see. Perhaps they didn't come across this sort of situation so they just looked for the obvious.

As for poor Nikki – wrong place, wrong time.

James arrived back at the motel at 1630 hours and packed his gear and checked out, paying for his room with his debit card. With a bit of luck he would be back in Hereford at about 2200.

Chapter 4

James was driving down the M40 en route to Hereford and it was raining hard. The water was running down the motorway and in the headlights you could imagine you were driving down a river. At the next services he pulled in. He was feeling tired and his stomach was rumbling.

Once inside he grabbed a tray and walked over to the counter. A young woman came over. She had black, shoulder-length hair. She was a little overweight but all the curves were in the right places and when she smiled her eyes lit up the room. She was very much alive.

'Can I help you?' she asked.

'You certainly can,' James replied though he really wasn't thinking about the food.

'Meat pudding, mash, peas, carrots and gravy, please.'

'Would you like a large one for the same price only it's been slow today and we have to throw what's left away in the morning.'

'Thank you, yes please.'

The meat pudding was piled on the plate with mash, carrots and peas.

'Would you like a couple of roast potatoes?'

'Thank you. They say the way to a man's heart is through his stomach.' James gave her a wicked smile. She covered the plate with gravy and placed it on the tray.

'Thank you.'

James moved down the counter. There was no one operating the coffee machine, so she said, 'I'll do that for you.'

'Coffee please.'

'Large or small?'

'Large, please.'

She poured the coffee and placed it on the tray. He moved on to the girl on the till.

'Maggie, charge the gentleman for normal size.'

While James was eating his dinner he looked around at the other customers just to see if there was a possible threat but there was none that he could see.

He finished his meal and was drinking the coffee when the girl from behind the counter came over and placed a cup of coffee on the table; she had another one in her hand.

'Do you mind if I sit here for a chat while I have my break?'

'No, help yourself.'

She sat down facing him with her cup of coffee on the table in front of her.

'What do you do for a living?' she asked.

'Commercial salesman.' Lie number one.

'How far have you got to go?'

'About sixty miles. I live at Hereford.'

'Do you mind if I ask you how old you are?'

'No, I'm twenty-nine. How old are you?'

'Twenty-four. Are you married?'

'Not any more. Divorced. It didn't work out for us. We were too young and I was away a lot of the time. Are you married or do you have a boyfriend?'

'I've never been married and I don't have a boyfriend at the moment. He was too possessive so I dumped him.'

'I've not even asked your name! I'm James.'

'My name is Candy.'

'That's a nice name, as sweet as sugar candy.'

Candy smiled at him and her eyes were sparkling.

'Do you come this way often?'

'Not really. Most of my work is in Midlands and the North.'

Lie number two. 'Your ex boyfriend must be stark raving mad to treat you like a possession. You belong to no one. You stay with someone because you want to.'

'I wasn't allowed to go out with my mates. He would have to come along and it would spoil everything.'

James put his hand in his pocket and pulled out his mobile phone. He passed it across the table. 'If you want to put your phone number in there and I'll give you a call and we could go out for a drink.'

She smiled, picked up the phone and entered Candy and the number and passed it back to him. She got up from the table with another smile.

'I had better get back. I hope to hear from you soon.'

'You will, I promise! I've got to go myself. See you soon. Bye.'

'I'll be waiting for your call. Bye.'

He gave her a smile and walked out to the car.

James arrived at the barracks at 2320 hours and flashed his ID card at the guard on the barrier. The trooper signed him in.

'Sergeant MacDonald, I have a message from Major Tompsett. He said if you came in tonight, would you see him in his office at 1000 hours tomorrow?'

Bloody keen! James thought. 'Thanks. Goodnight.'

'Goodnight, Sergeant.'

He returned to the car, parked up near his room and went inside. He grabbed his wash kit and took a shower. On his bed he lay looking at Stony's watch. Sleep didn't come easy. He lay there looking at the ceiling thinking of Stony, Bosnia and Jill and the murder. Then Candy came into his mind. He could do with her right now; there wouldn't be much talking going on. At last sleep came though it was of the restless kind.

At 0700 hours James was awakened by the alarm on Stony's watch. A quick shower and shave, then he got dressed in denim trousers and combat boots and a beret. He fancied a full English breakfast in the mess. James got his breakfast and was going to take it to a table when he heard a voice he knew.

'Hello, boy.' It was Ginger. 'I got back the day before yesterday. I was hoping to get back for the funeral. Tommo told me you went down. How's Jill?'

'She's coping, just. It's good to see you, Ginger. Where did they send you?'

'Just got back from Bosnia. Did you hear about Willie?'

'No, what? I only got back on duty on Monday.'

'Lost a foot on an anti-personnel mine. They're lying about like bloody confetti.'

'Have you heard how's he doing?'

'Fine, but he'll never soldier again unless they give him a desk job.'

'You know they're not for the likes of us. It's only the Ruperts who get offered a desk job.'

'You're right. The bastards!' Ginger took a swig of his coffee and looked at James. 'What have they put you on since you've been back?'

'All I got was to do the normal auction for Stony and the collection, then I went to the funeral. Only got back last night.'

'I'm away tomorrow to the Beacons,' Ginger said. 'Induction training for those who want to join the regiment.'

'I've a meeting with Tommo at 1000 hours. He might tell me what he wants me to do then.' James finished his coffee. 'How about meeting up in the mess tonight for a couple of pints?'

'OK, boy, but it should be a lot more than a couple. You're so bloody heavy, it was like carrying a horse.' They were both laughing their heads off.

'Say about 2000 hours?'

'Fine, see you then and bring some money!'

James got up and walked out of the mess and went over to the Adjutant's office to see Major Beech. Major Beech, or 'Woody' as he was known, happened to be talking to an orderly who was sitting at his desk. James was a rebel. Most of the time he would leave his beret off then he would not have to salute; he just stood to attention.

'Good morning, Sir,' he said.

'Good morning, Sergeant. Did you want to see me?'

'Just a quick one, Sir. I've a meeting with Major Tompsett at 1000 hours, so I've come to see if you've an ordinance survey map of the Maidstone area in Kent.'

'Yes, I'll send it over to Major Tompsett's office.'

'Thank you, Sir.'

James turned round and walked out of the office and sat on a bench to light up a cigarette and wonder how the meeting with Tommo would go down. James looked at his watch. Fifteen minutes to go. He stood up and put his cigarette out. He walked into the outer office with five minutes to go. The orderly stood up.

'Hello, Sergeant, you've a meeting with Major Tompsett. I'll tell him you are here. He has Hiccup with him at the moment.'

He picked up the telephone and rang through. Colonel George 'Hiccup' Hickly was the Commanding Officer and the biggest prick you could ever find; he had made so many mistakes which was why he was called Hiccup.

'You can go in now, Sergeant. By the way the adjutant sent these maps over for you.'

'Thanks.'

He put his beret on as the gaffer was in there. He knocked on the door and waited until asked to come in.

'Come in.'

James opened the door and went in, closing the door behind him. He turned to face the officers, stood to attention and saluted them.

He was offered a seat in front of the desk. He removed his beret and sat down.

'Sergeant MacDonald, can I have your report on Captain Burkes' death verbally now and in writing tomorrow?' Major Tompsett asked.

'Yes, Sir.' James cut to the chase. 'Sir, please can I ask what Captain Burkes' assignment was in Northern Ireland?'

'Who said he was in Ireland?' retorted Hiccup.

'I know he was in Northern Ireland. When I give you my report you'll see *how* I know.'

James looked at Hiccup with a look that said, 'It's going to be one of *those* meetings.'

'Captain Burke was murdered,' James went on.

'Do you have any proof, Sergeant?' Hiccup raised his voice.

'All the proof I need, Sir.'

'Well, let's get started with your report.'

'Can we go over to the map table, Sir?'

'Of course.'

They got up and went to the table. Hiccup was still like a bear with a sore head and James was beginning to enjoy himself. He spread the map across the table. He picked up a pencil to use as a pointer, then started the report.

'This is the crash site.' James pointed to the map. 'As you can see, the road there is a steep hill with banks on either side. Point one: Captain Burke had nowhere to go to avoid the lorry; if he had tried he would have turned the car over and taken all the impact.'

'That doesn't prove a thing.' Hiccup interrupted.

James continued. 'Can you see the winding road at the bottom of the hill and this bridge over the stream? When Captain Burkes' car reached the bridge the lorry was started from this point here.'

'Pure speculation!'

'I've checked it with the speeds the police gave me, Sir. It works out perfectly … See these bushes on this knoll. I found one that had been used as an observation point. You could see the road and the bridge from it.' James put his hand in his pocket and pulled out his cigarette packet.

'No smoking, Sergeant.'

'I wasn't going to, Sir.' James opened the packet and took out the cigar butt and passed it to him.

'Is there any way you can find out the make? I doubt if you'll find any DNA on it.'

'What has that got to do with anything?' *Bloody Hiccup again! – he was beginning to become a pain in the bum.*

'I found it in the observation post and I thought intelligence might find it useful. I want to find the Captain's murderers.'

'It's not about what *you* want, Sergeant.'

'No, Sir.'

'Do the police know all this?' Major Tompsett asked.

'No, Sir, I work for you and it's not my place to talk to the police, although Chief Inspector Reeves was very co-operative.'

'Can you wait in the outer office?'

'Yes, Sir.'

James stood up, replaced his beret, stood to attention, saluted and retreated to the outer office. He sat in a chair to wait to see what was going to happen next.

There was a lot of raised voices coming from the office but James and the orderly couldn't make out what they were saying. The orderly looked at James. 'Old Hiccups in one of his moods again, eh? Have you been rubbing him up the wrong way again?'

'I'm always rubbing him up the wrong way. He's an arrogant pig.'

After a while the door opened and the Commanding Office left the building, not saying a word to anyone.

Major Tompsett came to the door. 'Come in, Sergeant.' He

offered James a seat. 'Two coffees, please. One black no sugar and you know what I have,' he shouted back through the door.

'Yes, Sir,' the orderly replied.

'Thank you, James, for your report. You did a good job, very good, but you are like a red rag to a bull with the CO.'

'But he's a prick and I can't stand fools.'

'Look, James, Stony *was* in Ireland training the Green Jackets but his real job was to find out how the IRA was getting information on military movements. We've suffered a lot of casualties lately and we think we've got a mole and we want him badly alive or dead, preferably dead. Stony must have found out something or was getting too close and was taken out so we didn't receive any information. The end of next week you'll take his place. See me next Wednesday and I'll have everything arranged.'

'What time, Sir?'

'Ten hundred hours.'

'Fine.'

'The prick, as you call him, didn't want me to send you until I told him that Captain Burke must have been compromised so *you* had an excellent chance of not coming back. Then he said he would be happy to leave it in your capable hands.'

'Thanks a bunch! I'll do my best not to oblige him, Sir.'

'I think that's it for now.'

'Just one other thing, Sir. Chief Inspector Reeves has a shooting team and I told him that you could arrange a shooting competition at Hythe and lay on some refreshments. Can you give him a ring, Sir.'

'Leave it to me.'

'Thank you, Sir. See you on Wednesday.'

At 2000 hours James went to the mess. Ginger was sitting at the bar.

'Hello, boy, have they posted you yet?'

'No, the Major just wanted to know how the funeral went and what the police had to say. He also wants a written report tomorrow.'

'Don't they think it was an accident then?'

'The police do, I think. They just want a report on file.' Half true. 'Would you like your pint now?'

'Yes, please, then you've paid your debt in full.'

'It's just a pity I can't repay the debt I owe Stony. He saved my life. I know you helped a bit.'

'What do you mean a bit? Must have carried you three bloody miles.'

'Three bloody miles, my arse!'

'It was your bloody arse we saved!'

'Then I've overpaid you. It should have been a half a pint; it wasn't a very comfortable ride.'

'James, if you're going to be a skinflint, I'll not bother again. I'll leave you there to rot.'

'You know you wouldn't; you love me really.'

'How about a game of darts?' Ginger asked.

'I'll play you for a fiver a game.'

'You think I was born yesterday, I've seen the way you throw those bloody knives of yours.'

They played darts until 2300 hours and then they retired to their beds.

Chapter 5

Next morning James was up at 0600 hours. He got a pair of combat trousers out of his locker and a short-sleeved vest and threw them on the bed. He took a key off the windowsill and went back to his locker and undid the padlock on an old army ammunition tin box, to which he had welded a hasp and staple. He had also drilled two holes into the bottom and these matched up with holes in the bottom of the locker; two bolts with wing nuts held the box in place. The wing nuts meant that it could be removed without the use of tools.

He took out the two knives and strapped them to his legs. He then put his combat trousers on, checked the Velcro and made sure that the knives were in the right place. Finally he placed Stony's Walther and watch in the ammunition box and relocked it, put the keys in his trouser pocket. A clean pair of socks, then his boots, and he was ready.

It was still dark when he signed out at the guardhouse and then he was on his way jogging towards the A4399. There was hardly anyone around, just the odd person on their way to work or going home. At that time in the morning in September it was what he called a hop-picking morning: the dew made the ground damp and there was a chill in the air. The conditions were perfect. He got into his stride, his heart rate rising as he began to warm up.

Just before Mordford there was a small wood on the right and he turned up a track that went into the wood. He slowed to a walk because of all the ruts where a tractor had been driven up and down through the mud; he didn't want to risk a turned ankle or any other injury. After about one hundred and fifty metres he was in a clearing where all the trees had been cut down and taken away, all, that is, except one. James sat down on it.

James sat there for about a quarter of an hour, letting his heart rate return to normal. At the edge of the clearing he picked out a tree. He paced out six metres from the base of the tree and marked the ground by dragging the heel of his boot, and did the same at nine meters. He turned to face the tree and walked back to the six-metre mark, picked a spot on the tree at about two metres from the ground, then reached down to pull open the Velcro fastening on his trousers. In one movement he grabbed the knife and threw it at the tree. A second later it struck the tree with a thud at exactly the right spot.

He made a grab with his left hand, opened the Velcro, took out the knife, transferred it to his right and threw it. It landed in the tree alongside the first knife. He smiled. He hated it if he missed the tree, not that he missed very often. After retrieving the knives he walked to the nine-metre mark and repeated the exercise. This time he was a little low – he had not allowed enough height for the extra distance. He pulled out the knives and tried again. This time he was bang on target.

James spent the next half an hour throwing some underarm and some sideways which meant that the blade was parallel to the ground. This was more difficult but they still hit the tree on target. When he had finished he put the knives away and did up the Velcro on his trousers and made sure it didn't show.

James walked back down the track to the main road and started jogging towards Mordford. He was in a very good mood and once through Mordford he stayed on the main road and went back into Hereford.

* * *

Later that day after dinner James walked into Major Tompsett's office. In the outer office he saw the orderly.

'Major Tompsett, please.'

'Can you wait a while? He's with Hiccup.'

'That's fine. I'll wait.'

James took a seat and after about a quarter of an hour later Major Tompsett appeared out of the CO's office which was opposite his own.

'Do you want to see me?'

'Yes, Sir.'

'It will have to be quick; I've another appointment.'

James followed him into his office. 'Sir, I was wondering if it would be possible as I'm away across the water shortly if I could have a couple of days off?'

'As you are only doing fitness training I'll put you down as on call – as long as you keep up the training.'

'Thank you, Sir.'

'How is the training going anyway?'

'Fine, Sir, I did ten Ks this morning and no ill effects.'

'By the way that cigar butt you gave me – there was no DNA that could be taken off it.'

'That was quick, Sir.'

'The make of the cigar is Meharis. It's a Dutch brand.'

'Thank you, Sir.'

'I've also spoken to Chief Inspector Reeves and he spoke very highly of you.'

'He's a good man. Can we change him for the CO, Sir.'

'No.'

'That's a pity.'

'I've arranged the shoot but I'm afraid you won't be on it; you'll be in Ireland or dead.'

'That would make Hiccup's day.'

'I'll see you on Wednesday. Enjoy yourself.'

'Thanks again, Sir. Goodbye.' Smiling, James stood to attention and turned and walked out of the office. He was still smiling when he walked past the orderly.

'You look like the cat that got the cream.'

'Something like that.'

James sat on his bench and put his hand in his pocket and pulled out his mobile phone. He pushed the menu button, flicked through to stored numbers, found Candy and pushed the dial button.

'Hello.'

'Hello, is that Candy?'

'Yes.'

'This is James. Can you talk?'

'Yes, it's nice to hear your voice.'

'Why I phoned is because I've to go to Scotland soon and I don't know how long I'll be away for but I've a couple of days off and was hoping that we might go out.'

'I'm working until nine.'

'How about if I pick you up from work and we go for a drink?'

'Yes, that will be very nice. I look forward to seeing you again. Must go now. See you later, bye.'

He pushed the end of call button and walked smartly back to his room, got a case down from off the top of his locker, opened it up on the bed and packed it with casual clothes.

It was 2000 hours when he pulled into the services. He got out of the car and left the flowers he had bought in the back – he didn't want to embarrass Candy. Candy was standing behind the hot food counter, her eyes met his and she gave him a smile.

'You're early,' she said.

'I know, I thought I would have a dinner while waiting. Anyway I would be happy to sit here and look at you all night.'

'You've a smooth tongue. What do you want?'

'I'll tell you later.'

'Food I meant.' Her face turned slightly red but her eyes were twinkling and the smile grew bigger.

'Oh, what is the fish?'

'Cod in batter but if you don't behave yourself it will be a bloody goldfish.'

Candy dished up the food and gave him the biggest bit of fish that was there and handed him the plate.

'Thanks. I'll sit at that table then I can keep an eye on you.'

'Go on with you.'

He pushed the tray down to the till and paid for the food. 'Your mate's nice,' he said to the girl. 'Do you think she would go out with me?'

She started to giggle. 'I don't know.'

During his meal he spotted Candy and the girl were talking and laughing together. James guessed what they were talking about. Clearly the girl didn't know about the date.

The girl came over to the table. 'Is your dinner OK, Sir.'

'Very, very nice.'

'I asked her if she would like to go out with you and she said, "He's not my type, too much up his own arse."'

'That's not very nice, is it?'

'No, it's not.'

'What's *your* name?'

'Helen.'

'Helen, will *you* come out with me?'

The girl went back to the till, looked at Candy and smiled.

James looked at Candy, gave her a smile and a wink; she smiled back at him. James looked at his watch. It was ten minutes to zero. He waited as Candy went and got her coat and came over to the table and grabbed James by the arm and led him out via the till. She waved to the girl and James put up his thumb.

'You had it arranged all the time!' Helen said, giggling again.

'You're right. Goodnight.'

'Goodnight, Helen,' James said. 'And I hope it's a goodnight.'

'How do you know her name?'

'I asked her out after you said you didn't want to go out with me.'

'You bugger!' She gave him a right hook.

In the car James turned to give her a kiss on the cheek but she saw it coming. She turned her head and kissed him full on the lips. He wrapped his arms around her and gave her another kiss.

'Let's find a hotel and I'll book in.'

'No need to. I live on my own and have my own flat. You can stop with me.'

'Are you sure?'

'Yes.'

'OK. Now where shall we get this drink?'

'The Henchman. It's near where I live.'

'Right,' James started the engine. 'You can give me directions.'

At the pub James went to the bar and ordered a vodka and orange and half a lager. He had chosen a table where he could watch both the bar and the door. This was just instinctive because across the water you were just as likely to get shot in a pub, bar or club as you would on the street.

'What do you like doing?' he asked.

'I like dancing and going to nightclubs but I've something to tell you first.'

'Go on then.'

'I tried to get a couple of days off but I couldn't manage it. I managed to change shifts, though, so we can spend the afternoons and evenings together.'

'That's nice of you.'

'Now I'll answer your question fully: I like walking my favourite walk down by the river and going to the cinema. When have you got to go to Scotland?'

'I've to see the boss on Wednesday morning at ten.' Lie one.

'You said you were a sales rep. What do you sell?'

'Farm tractors and machinery, not to the farmers but to the distributors; that's why I travel all over Britain.' Lie two.

'Would you like another drink?' James asked.

'No thank you. Let's get a bottle of wine and take it home and we can have a drink there.'

James went to the bar and asked if they sold wine by the bottle. He picked a bottle of sparkling white wine.

'Will this one do?'

Candy took hold of the bottle. 'Yes this is fine. I like Concord.'

Outside in the car park, as he put the wine on the back seat, James gave Candy the flowers.

'Beautiful flowers for a beautiful lady.'

'Oh thank you, James! They're beautiful.' She was wiping a tear from her eye.

'Why are you crying? I thought you would be pleased.'

'Oh it's just that this was the last thing I was expecting. You didn't strike me as the flower type.'

'Well, what type would you say I was?'

'The strong silent type, hard as nails, who hides any fears or worries, and nobody knows what he's feeling.'

'You've got me taped.'

'Let's go home.'

A little later James followed her into a block of ordinary-looking flats, up a flight of stairs, along a corridor until they reached a door with number six on it.

The flat was tiny but spotless. You could tell it had a lady owner because of the fresh smell and the shelves full of toiletries in the small, neat bathroom. In the living room he put down his case and the bottle of wine on a coffee table. The room was sparsely decorated. She had a television in one corner with a DVD player and video recorder underneath; she also had a music centre in the other corner. The only other furniture was a small three-piece suite.

Candy turned on the television. 'I'm going to have a quick shower. Make yourself at home.'

As she went to the bathroom she turned around. 'By the way in the kitchen drawer by the cooker you'll find a corkscrew and the cupboard above is where the glasses are kept.'

James uncorked the wine and poured out two glasses and placed them on the coffee table. 'Have you got a vase,' James called through the bathroom door. 'I'll put the flowers in water.'

'There is one on the windowsill in the kitchen,' she shouted back through the sound of running water.

Once he had finished arranging them he put them on the windowsill in the living room.

After showering she came out of the bathroom wearing a white towelling dressing gown and went into the bedroom. After about three minutes later she came back into the living room. James looked at her with his mouth wide open. She was wearing a pink low-cut see-through nightdress which finished four or five inches above the knee. The nightdress clung to every curve and her nipples were trying to come out to play. She took a glass of wine and sat on the settee beside him.

'My God, you're beautiful.'

She lifted her legs and laid them across his lap, and as she did so the nightdress rode up exposing more leg. He placed his hand on her knee and started stroking her legs gently. She lowered one foot to the floor, which made her legs part, and he started stroking the inside of them, gradually moving higher until his fingers were exploring her bush. He found the lips and he slowly opened them and pushed a finger inside. She was purring like a kitten and her body shuddered.

James pushed it right in and started moving it slowly and then faster and faster. Candy gave out a scream but it wasn't a scream of pain, but of sheer joy.

Candy put her glass on the table, placed one leg either side of his then sat facing him. She took off his sweatshirt and threw it on to the floor. She gasped. His body was all muscle, then she noticed that he had a scar that ran right across his body.

'Bloody hell, what happened there?'

'A fight in a pub.'

'Where did it happen?'

'Manchester.'

'What caused it?'

'A knife.'

Candy ran her fingers over the scar as if she was trying to heal it, but it had healed a long time ago. She took off her nightdress and threw it on top of the sweatshirt. She pulled his head towards her breasts, and he started licking and sucking her nipples. They were responding and getting bigger and harder, and she was making contented noises. She jumped up and pulled him off the settee and took him to the bedroom. James kicked off his shoes. She whipped off his trousers and boxers and pushed him on to the bed then jumped on top of him, one leg either side. She lowered herself until he was just at the entrance.

'What about a condom?'

'Shh, I'm on the pill.'

James arched his back to try to go deeper inside her. She pulled away so it was still at the entrance then she dropped down and started to ride him like a horse, slowly at first and then getting faster. Candy's breasts were bouncing about so James held them and rubbed his thumbs over the nipples, then all of a sudden she shouted out loud.

'Oh my God, Oh my God, I've got it! … Oh!' She collapsed and lay still on top of him, her breasts squashed against his chest. He was still inside her so he made his cock twitch.

'Stop it!' she giggled.

James did it again.

'Bastard!'

Candy rolled off and lay beside him. 'I needed that! Do you know that's the first time I've had an orgasm that felt as if it would never stop. If it had carried on, it would have driven me mad.'

'What do you mean, *driven* you mad? You're mad already.'

She gave him a black look so he grabbed her and gave her a long lingering kiss. His tongue parted her lips then they lay in each other's arms.

'Lets have a shower together,' she said and got off the bed. James followed her to the bathroom. In the shower he let the water run all over them. He then got the shower gel, squeezed it onto a sponge and soaped her all over, and then she did the same to him.

'You're all scars! How did you get that one? That's a bad wound and it's not all that old.'

'I was helping a friend and the ladder slipped. I fell on a spiked fence and the spike went right through. I came out of hospital six weeks ago.' Another bloody lie but what else could he do?

After they had dried themselves, James poured two glasses of wine and they climbed into bed, holding each other close.

'That's a night I shall never forget. Thank you, James.'

'I won't forget either. I've never met anyone like you.'

'What? Randy?'

'Beautiful, fun to be with, eyes that sparkle, very much alive, young and, of course, randy.'

James lay on his side with his knees up and Candy backed up close to him. He put one arm under her head with his hand holding her breast and the other arm over the top of her. She didn't say anything but she felt loved, safe and secure. Nothing could hurt her now; she was soon asleep.

At 0500 the alarm clock went off. Candy put her arm out of the bed and groped for the alarm clock and pushed the stop button and turned to James and kissed him. He responded by giving her a passionate kiss.

'Do you want me to take you to work?'

'No, a mate is picking me up.'

'I'll make you a drink. Tea or coffee? Would you like some toast?'

'No toast, but I'll have a cup of coffee. White no sugar.'

As she sipped her drink, she was still yawning. 'Can you pick me up at one, please.'

'Yes of course I can, but you're heavy – I won't have to carry you too far, will I?'

'What's that supposed to mean?'

'Well, you said pick me up.'

'It's too early in the morning for me to get jokes.'

'What would you like to do this afternoon?'

'If it's fine we could go down by the river and I'll show you my favourite place.'

'OK, I'll arrange a picnic.'

'Sounds fun.' She went to her handbag and gave him a spare key to the flat. 'Here you are. You can let yourself back in then.'

'Thanks. By the way, what's the address? I might not be able to find my way back.'

Candy smiled. 'You've only been here one night and that was in the dark. It's 6 St Peter's Drive, Chalfont.'

A car pulled up outside. 'I must go. See you at one.'

She kissed him, then as she went out of the door James called, 'See you later.'

James made another black coffee, washed up the cup that Candy had used and the two wine glasses, put them away, made the bed and picked up the nightdress and laid it neatly on the bed.

He sat watching television but after about half an hour he was bored. He picked up Candy's spare key and put it on the key ring with his car keys.

Out in the courtyard a lady was pulling a shopping trolley. A packet of cornflakes was sticking out of the top.

'Excuse me, love, could you tell me the way to the local shops?'

'Yes, young man,' she replied, 'Turn left at the end of this road, then turn left again at…' She was thinking and counting on her fingers. 'Yes, take the third turning left, go along there; you'll come to a park, go across the park and out through the main gate, turn left and the shops are about fifty yards down.'

'Thank you very much. How far away are they?'

'About half a mile I would say but you can get a bus at the top of this road – the number 33.'

'Thank you very much.'

James set off at a brisk pace and once at the park he started to jog, passing about half a dozen young mums playing with their toddlers in the play area, and a few people walking their dogs. He recalled the lady's instructions. Out through the main gate. Turn left. The shops could now be seen. He spotted the Co-op. That will do. He picked up a basket and made his way along the shelves. Picnic food – bread, eggs, butter, tin of tuna, cucumber, box of cress, tomatoes, Scotch eggs. She already had milk in the fridge. Last but not least a bottle of white wine with a screw top. At the checkout he packed the goods into plastic bags. Out came the debit card.

'Would you like any cashback?' the checkout girl asked.

'Yes five grand will do.'

'You'll be lucky.'

'I take that as a no then.'

She was still laughing when James signed the slip.

'I'm glad I've made your day, goodbye.'

'Goodbye.'

She was still laughing as he went out of the door.

Once back at the flat James made himself busy making the sandwiches. He found a flask and filled it with black coffee. He also found a small jar that he filled with milk. A picnic hamper was out of the question, but he remembered spotting a suitcase on top of the wardrobe. Bingo! He packed it with the sandwiches, flask, two cups and two glasses, tomatoes and Scotch eggs.

At the services Candy was already waiting outside. She was smiling. 'Do you want the good news or the bad news?'

'Good news first.'

'I've managed to change shifts so I don't have to go into work tomorrow.'

'And the bad news?'

'You'll have to put up with me all day and night.'

'That *is* bad news.'

Candy punched him in the arm. 'You are a sod.'

'Not really. Now show me this river you keep talking about.'

About half an hour later they were in a car park. The river was close by at the bottom of a bank of grass. James got the picnic case out of the boot and found about two metres of string, he rolled it up and put it in his pocket.

'Candy, there's a car rug on the back seat. Can you get it, please?'

He locked the car. She grabbed his hand. 'This way!'

They walked along the riverbank past moorings with houseboats and motor boats.

After another two hundred metres or so the moorings had finished and it was just the river with open countryside on either side of the river. They walked another half a mile and they came to a cut-out in the bank.

'They were done for fishing but anyone can use them.'

Candy climbed down the bank and on to the flat area and laid the rug out on the ground. James followed her and put the 'picnic basket' down. He took the string out of his pocket, tied one end to the branch of a bush and the other end to the bottle of wine and lowered it into the river.

'See, I've my own fridge.'

'You're mad.'

'You'll not think that when we have chilled wine.'

He sat down on the rug and she lay down with her head on his lap. As he looked at the river and the countryside, he placed his hand on the side of her face and ran his fingers through her hair.

'That's nice. Don't stop.'

'It's very nice here. It's got everything. It's quiet. There's a view, water lapping against the bank and a beautiful woman … Heaven!'

'I'm in heaven too, just being here with you.'

James opened the case. 'What would you like to eat? I've tuna and cucumber, or egg and cress sandwiches.'

'I'll have one of each, please.'

'Would you like a Scotch egg and a tomato?

'Yes, please.'

He put them on a plate and passed them to her.

'Thank you.'

After they had finished eating, Candy laid back again and closed her eyes. He picked a piece of long grass and tickled her under the nose and took it away quickly. Her hand rubbed her nose and then settled down again, and again he tickled her with the grass. She opened her eyes quickly and knew instantly what he had done. She jumped up quickly.

'You're a very …'

That was as far as she got because he pulled her down and kissed her passionately on the lips and held her gently and firmly in his arms. They lay like that for a long while, then

James got up and went to the river and pulled up the bottle of wine. He poured two glasses.

'I told you, I've my own fridge.'

'It's lovely and cold.'

'What would you like to do tonight?'

'There are no discos tonight and the film that's on at the cinema I've seen before, so let's go to my place and watch a film or play some music and then get a takeaway later.'

'Sounds good to me. I could do with a shower just to see how many bites I've got.'

'Gnat bites?'

'No yours.'

'You're asking for it!'

'Yes, please.'

'Come on! Before I beat you up.'

Back at the flat James went into the bedroom, took a towel and clean boxers from his case and went and had a shower. When he went back into the living room, Candy had been in the bedroom and put on her nightdress and was standing there looking through CDs. Without looking up she picked one and slotted it into the CD player. She turned to James.

'Will you dance with me?'

'Yes of course I will.'

As the music started to play he put his arms around her and held her bottom as they began to dance. The music was 'The Wind beneath My Wings'. He looked down at her. Her eyes were closed.

The music had finished so she replaced the CD. She started dancing on her own and, as she swayed, the nipples rubbed against her nightdress. Finally she knelt on the settee with her hands on the back. Her legs were open and there was a welcome to the world of pleasure.

'Take me.'

James took off his boxers, stood behind and guided himself in. He held her breasts and started moving in and out. She was moaning and groaning. He moved faster and faster, her body started to shudder and they both climaxed together. She let out a scream and collapsed on the settee, with her head resting on her arm. Her eyes were closed.

James sat back in one of the chairs looking at her. Her vagina was still winking at him and his semen was leaking on to the settee. He grabbed his boxers and started to wipe her gently.

'Not now. It's too sensitive.'

'OK. I'll leave my boxers on the settee so it won't muck it up.'

Candy stayed there for a while, then she looked at James with tears in her eyes.

'Why are you crying?'

'I don't want this moment to end; I want it to go on for ever and ever. I'm in love with you!'

'Did I hear you right?'

'Yes I love you, I love you. I know it's only been a couple of days but I know I want to be with you always.'

James walked over and threw the boxer shorts on the floor and sat on the settee alongside her.

'You won't even like me when you know that I've lied to you all the way along.'

'You *are* married.'

'No, just listen. There are a hundred and one good reasons why we shouldn't be together.'

Tears were rolling down her cheeks and dripping on to her thighs. 'You're going to dump me?'

'I'm only thinking of you. I promised myself I wouldn't get into another relationship again, just casual ones.' He held her hand and looked into her eyes. They were red and she was sobbing her heart out.

'Look at me! I'm not a tractor salesman; I'm a sergeant in the SAS. That scar on my leg wasn't done by a fence spike; it was done by a bullet. And the scar on my belly was from a knife fight in Ireland. I could have to go anywhere in world at the drop of a hat and you wouldn't know where I was or when I would be coming home. One of these days I'll meet someone who's faster, stronger and quicker than me, and then I won't come home at all. How would you be able to cope with all that pressure? You would soon find someone else.'

'I know it seems as if I'm throwing myself at you but I do know how I feel and I promise I would never leave you.'

'You say that now but I'm not going to Scotland and I can't tell you when I'll be back, or where I am going.'

'James, I do understand. I'm not a kid! Do you have any feelings for me?'

'I think you're one of the best things that has happened to me, ever.'

'I'm no angel, I'm not a virgin but I would never ever cheat on you. I understand what you've said and I'll prove to you over time that I would be good for you. Are … are you going to leave?'

'Go and have a shower and give me time to think, then I'll give you my answer.'

She ran to the bathroom and James could hear the shower going and sat thinking quietly. When she was dry she came back in the living room. She was still naked.

'Well, have you got an answer?'

'Yes I have an answer. I've told you all the conditions that will have to apply, so will you be my girl?'

Candy threw her arms around and clung on tight.

'You won't be sorry! Not ever, I promise.'

'Can I pick a CD?'

'Of course.'

It was 'I'm in Love with a Beautiful Woman'.

'Can I have this dance?'

'Yes.'

She jumped up straight into his arms. He held her close to

him as they danced and his old boy was rubbing against her belly button.

'I love you, James! You'll never know how much.'

'I love you too – very much.'

Next morning James was awake first. Very carefully he took off her signet ring from her engagement finger, got up and then put it in his trouser pocket. It was an hour before Candy got up.

'Been up long? You should have woken me up.'

'I knew you needed your beauty sleep.'

'You pig!'

'You'll do for me.' He kissed her.

'I've to go out for a while. I'll be about forty-five minutes.'

'Where are you going?'

'You should know better than to ask?'

'I understand. I'll have breakfast ready when you get back.'

He kissed her and said, 'See you!' And then he was gone.

He jogged back to the high street he had visited the day before. He remembered there had been a jeweller's.

'Good morning, Sir.'

'Good morning, can you show some engagement rings?'

'What price range?'

'Say three to five hundred.'

The salesman went away and after a minute returned with three trays and placed them on the counter. James picked a ring that had a bigger diamond in the middle and smaller ones around it; it looked like a flower.

'How much is this one?'

'That is a very good ring, Sir. It's priced at five hundred and thirty pounds, but well worth it.'

'It's thirty pounds over budget. Can you do anything about the thirty pounds, call it five hundred dead?'

'I'll not be a minute.'

He went out to the backroom and he could hear voices. The salesman returned to the counter.

'I had to ask Mr Biggs. He said yes.'

James pulled the ring out of his pocket. 'That's the size I require.'

The salesman picked up a ring gauge and measured the internal diameter of the ring.

'Look at that! The one you were looking at is the exact size.'

'If I keep the paperwork, can she change it if she doesn't like it?'

'That will be fine, Sir.'

Out came the good old plastic. The salesman put the ring in a box and handed to him.

'Just keep the receipt, Sir.'

Back at the flat Candy had breakfast ready – eggs, bacon, sausages, beans and a fried slice – and as soon as he walked in he could smell it. It made his mouth water.

'Brilliant, it's better than the takeaway that we were going to have last night, remember.'

She laughed. 'We never did get one, did we?'

'No, we were too busy.'

They sat at the kitchen table and started their breakfast.

'Now tell me about yourself. You're a woman of mystery; I don't even know your surname! I'm Sergeant James MacDonald.'

'Candice Martin, but I like to be called Candy.'

'Nice to meet you, Candy.'

'Now tell me all about yourself.'

'Not much to tell really. My mother died when I was twelve and I went to live with my nan, I lived with my nan for four years, until I was sixteen, and then my father got married again and didn't want me to live with him. I managed to get a job as a childminder and lived in. The hours were long and I didn't go out much so I saved some money. Then the job came up at the services and I rented this place.'

After breakfast James took a bottle of wine out of the fridge and two glasses and they went back to the spot by the river. It was a beautiful sunny day. Surreptitiously James tied the ring on to the end of the string that was still hanging on the bush, then he tied the bottle of wine on to the string close to the ring so when it was pulled out later it would be seen.

After about an hour he gave Candy a nudge. 'Get the wine, babe, it should be cold by now.'

Candy got up, went over to the string and slowly pulled it out of the water. He heard her gasp.

'What's this?'

'Will you marry me, Candice Martin?'

'Do you mean it? You're not having a laugh.'

'I'll ask you again: will you marry me?'

'Yes. Yes. Yes!'

Her hands were shaking as she fumbled with the string trying to untie the knot. After what seemed like ages she managed to get the ring and put it on her finger. She came over and sat by James. She was just sitting there staring at the ring.

'I can't believe it! It's beautiful and I'm engaged to be Mrs James MacDonald.'

'I only hope that I can make you very happy.'

'You will! You've made me happy already, and I promise you that I'll always be there for you. I love you.'

'I'm sorry but you know I'm away tomorrow and I've a lot to sort out. You'll have to live at Hereford and it will be a long engagement. Do you mind?'

'I know. I'd move anywhere. I just want to be with you always and for ever.'

Suddenly she realised her signet ring was missing. 'I've lost my signet ring!'

'No, you haven't. It's on the bedside table. I needed it to get the right size ring.'

'Remind me not to play cards with you. You're sneaky.'

'How about a game of strip poker?'

'Any time.'

'It will have to wait; I've not got a pack of cards with me.'

'Can we go to the services and have something to eat. I want to show my ring off.'

'You're not going to drop your knickers, are you?'

'What do you mean?'

'You said you were going to show your ring off.'

'You're sex mad.'

'I know but look who's talking.'

'Six of one, half a dozen of the other.'

When they got to the services Candy said, 'You go and sit at a table and I'll get the dinner and bring it over. What would you like?'

'You choose.'

'All right.'

Candy was showing them all her engagement ring. She was as happy as a dog with two tails both wagging. A lady in her mid-forties came over with a steak-and-kidney pie on a tray and placed it in front of him. She was a big lady with massive boobs and reminded him of a hospital matron.

'Congratulations, I'm Mary. She's a lovely girl and she deserves some luck.'

'I'm James.'

'You seem to care a lot for her.'

'Yes I do.'

'How long have you known her?'

'Three days.'

'Three days! Are you two mad?'

'Yes, but does she look happy?'

'Radiant and so very much alive but I don't want her to get hurt. She finished with her boy friend a little while ago and he was a right bastard.'

'I'm glad you care. Will you do me a favour? I have to go away for a while; will you look out for her?'

54

'Too right I will. I'd better get back now.'

'Bye, Mum.'

'Cheeky devil!'

James had finished his food and was drinking his coffee. Candy was eating her meal behind the counter. She waved and shouted, 'Won't be long.'

He smiled and waved back. Eventually she came over, kissed him then grabbed his hand.

'Let's go home. I'm so very happy. Thank you!'

On the way out she bumped into Helen and showed her the ring.

'Congratulations, it's beautiful.'

'You might have got one but you turned me down the other night,' James quipped.

Candy gave him a slap. 'You wait till I get you home.'

When they got back to the flat she was still like a dog with two tails. She sat on his lap and he stroked her back and then he started kissing her neck. She was getting all twitchy.

'What time have we got to get up in the morning?

'I have to leave at six.'

'I'll set the alarm for five, OK?'

'When we're married, can we have kids … not straight away, but later. I would love to have kids with you.'

'Don't move too fast. Let's see if it works first.'

'It's going to work; I know it will because I love you so much. Thank you for taking a chance with me.'

'It's not *me* taking a chance; it's both of us.'

'Let's go to bed: early to bed, early to rise.'

'No, I'll rise tonight.'

In the bedroom he started to fondle her and then rolled on top. She guided him in and the bed started to move up and down. The rhythm got faster and faster and then she arched her back and screamed.

'You've brought me to a climax every time.'

'You're just lucky.'

They just lay there wrapped in each other's arms and fell asleep happy and contented.

In the morning James packed his case while Candy made the coffee. He held her hands.

'Now look after yourself and remember I love you and I'll ring you as soon as I can. If you ever feel down, look at your ring.'

'James, I love you.'

They kissed and then he was gone.

Chapter 6

Ten hundred hours and Sergeant James MacDonald was sitting in the outer office waiting to see Major Tompsett.

'Anybody in with the Major?'

'No, Sergeant, but he knows you're here.'

Thank God the CO wasn't with him! Maybe he would get an easy ride. Another ten minutes passed. Bloody hell! Hiccup came out of his office and went into the Major's office. Thought it was too good to be true. The phone rang on the Corporal's desk. He picked up the receiver and answered it.

'You can go in now, Sergeant.'

'Thank you. Wish me luck. I've got a feeling I'm going to need it.'

In front of the desk he stood to attention and saluted.

'Good morning, Sergeant.'

'Good morning, Sir.'

'Take a seat, Sergeant.'

James took off his beret and sat down in the chair in front of the desk; he placed the beret on his knee.

Hiccup looked James straight in the eyes, with a peculiar sneer on his face. 'We've read your report on the death of Captain Burke and his daughter Nikki and we've come to the conclusion that there is not enough evidence that he was killed unlawfully so it is left on file that the case is closed and that his death was a tragic accident.'

James sat there, his blood beginning to boil.

'Accident my foot, Sir. There is more than enough evidence in that report. It all adds up to the IRA.'

Major Tompsett defused the situation by picking up a file and laying it on his desk. 'Sergeant MacDonald, you'll report to Colonel Wiseman or Major Franklin of the Royal Green Jackets at Armagh Barracks. You'll train their young soldiers.'

'Not childminding, Sir?'

James was still hot under the collar and shouldn't have opened his mouth.

'Just listen, Sergeant.'

'Yes Sir.'

'That is your cover story, although you'll have to do enough of the training to be believed. We want you find out where the IRA is getting its vital information from and stop it. It could be that their intelligence is getting better, but we think it could be an internal mole. We're taking a lot more casualties than we've ever experienced during the last three months.'

Colonel Hiccup looked at his watch, stood up and said to Major Tompsett. 'I'll leave you to finish off; I've another appointment in ten minutes' time.'

He walked out without saying a word to either of them, and with a face like thunder.

'What's the history between you and the Colonel?'

'About two years ago I asked for a night extraction at 0430 hours; the helicopter arrived at 0930 hours in broad daylight. We were shot to pieces and we lost three men. When we got back, we unloaded our dead and I went to the pilot. I blew my top. He told me that Colonel Hickly had ordered him to fly him and an American general to a meeting. They could have driven to it because it wasn't even behind enemy lines; he just wanted to show off and it cost three good men their lives.'

'I didn't know any of this.'

'He doesn't care about any of his men, Sir. Just look at Stony. Even if it had to be for operational reasons, an open verdict would have been better. Jill could have a widow's pension.'

'I can see that you've a real hatred for the Colonel.'

'Now you know why, when you said there was a good chance I wouldn't come back, he jumped at the chance to send me.'

'Let's get back to business, James. Here's a list of contacts and numbers. Take all the gear you want over to the armoury and leave it with the armourer and draw the weapons and equipment you need, and, by the way, good luck and stick to the rules.'

'What rules? Yours or mine?'

'What's your rules?'

'Kill or be killed.'

'Better stick to mine – the green card.'

James was laughing.

'That's the rules that send us out with one hand tied behind our backs.'

'By the way, how was your couple of days off? Did you get plenty of exercise?'

'Oh yes, Sir.'

'Do me a favour, Major. Tell the Colonel I'll see him sometime.'

'Good luck again, James. See you soon.'

'OK, Sir. Thank you.'

James stood to attention, turned and walked out of the office and back to his room. He took the key out of his pocket and unlocked the ammunition box, undid the wing nuts and removed the box from the locker and put it on the bed. He opened the lid to check the contents, black Gortex suit, black balaclava, two 9-mm pistols, two strap-on knives and a belt knife, a cheese wire, two hundred rounds of 9-mm ammunition, a compass and a torch with tape across the glass so it only gave a very small area of light. Then he got out two suitcases, one from on top of his locker and the other he had used the last couple of days. James opened the case he had taken to Candy's. Inside was a piece of folded paper: 'All my love now and for ever, from your girl, Candy xxxx.'

James smiled, kissed the piece of paper and put it in the ammunition box.

Having packed his gear, he went off to the armoury. He was greeted by Bullet, the armourer.

'Hi, James, I've had a phone call from the old man. If you put all your gear down there I'll make sure it gets loaded on the chopper. Can you sign for the SA80? It's a good one. I've cleaned and oiled it and all the working parts have been checked. The magazine and ammunition I'll pack in your webbing. Is there anything else you need?'

'Have you got a spare Claymore?'

'That's a naughty one to ask for.'

'I know.'

'You know I shouldn't, but for The Shadow I'll make an exception. I'll put it straight in your box.'

James opened the box and locked the Claymore away.

'Thanks. See you later.'

'Later,' Bullets replied.

At 1645 hours, James was back at the armoury. The helicopter was on the ground waiting. James saw Bullet.

'Everything is on board, except for this.' He cocked the weapon. Holding the working parts to the rear, he tilted it so James could see inside.

'Clear,' James said.

Bullet let the working parts go forward, fired and put the safety catch on and handed it to James.

'Thanks for all you've done.'

'You're more than welcome. See you.'

James walked over to the helicopter and got on board.

Meanwhile over in Armagh Barracks Colonel Wiseman was on the telephone to Major Tompsett on a secure line.

'Colonel, a Sergeant James MacDonald will be arriving

tonight by helicopter. Estimated time of arrival 2000 hours. Will you arrange for pickup? The pilot will radio in when he requires ground defence.'

'Yes, I'll have it all arranged. Is he a good soldier, Major?'

'One of the best. He's only twenty-nine and already holds the DSC and the MM. He was wounded in Bosnia, only been out of hospital six weeks.'

'He sounds too good to be true, Major.'

'It's true, Colonel, he won't do everything by the book, but he gets results and that's all we need. Can you make sure he gets all help and equipment he needs?'

'Yes, Major, I'll see to it now and I'll see him in my office in the morning.'

Colonel Wiseman picked up the internal telephone and dialled a number and Major Franklin picked up the phone.

'Hello, this is Major Franklin.'

'Major, can you come to my office as soon as possible?'

'Yes, Sir, on my way.' He replaced the receiver, picked up his beret and walked to the Colonel's office. He saluted.

'You wanted to see me, Sir.'

'Major Tompsett has been on the telephone and we've a replacement, an SAS sergeant. He's arriving tonight at 2000 hours. What section is on call?'

'Corporal Brown's section, Sir.'

'Will you arrange for Corporal Brown to draw a three-toner from the motor pool and take his section to bring him in and get him settled in. He can have Captain Burke's old room. Tell the Corporal to show him where everything is and we'll see him in the morning at 0930 hours. You can see him at the same time.'

'Sure, I'll sort it out straight away, Sir, and I'll see you at 0930. Goodnight, Sir.'

'Alpha one four, this is Juliet two zero.'

'Hello, Juliet two zero.'

'Alpha one four, can you secure landing and a quick

unload please. I don't want this bird on the ground too long.'

'Corporal Brown, ten minutes and the pilot wants a quick turnaround.'

'I'm not going to hang about out there.'

Corporal Brown ran to the army lorry and jumped in the cab alongside the driver; the rest of the section was in the back. The engine burst into life and when they were through the gate they turned left. Another fifty metres they turned left again and were bouncing across a field. They stopped, jumped out and formed an all-round defence in front of the lorry. The second-in-command stayed in the rear and set up the General Purpose Machine Gun to cover the rear.

In the helicopter James had put his webbing on and taking a magazine out of the pouch he loaded it into the SA80 ready to go.

Back on the ground the section heard the helicopter's engine and rotors getting louder and the pilot sat it down in front of the lorry. The helicopter door opened and three of the section ran over and grabbed James' gear and put it in the back of the lorry. James jumped out and put his thumb up to the pilot, then sprinted to the lorry. The pilot opened the throttle up and was away. The lorry was racing back to the barracks and once through the gate it parked by the Motor Transport shed. They all jumped out and Corporal Brown went over to James.

'Sergeant MacDonald, I'm Corporal Brown. Welcome to Armagh Barracks. The Major has asked me to look after you and show you where everything is. I'll take you to your room first and get your equipment put in there.

'Thank you, Corporal, have any of your men got a round in the breach?'

'No, Sergeant.'

'Well, they can take their magazines out and put them away without going to the unloading bay.'

After they had taken their magazines out and replaced them in their pouches, Corporal Brown asked James to follow him. They went to a small room with a bed and a locker, not big enough to swing a cat, but it was to be his home all the time he was there. Three soldiers had his gear and put it down by the locker.

'Thanks, lads.' They turned and walked away.

'Corporal, is there anywhere we can get something to eat? I could eat a horse.'

'You won't get a horse, Sergeant. At this time of night it will be something with chips.'

'That will do. Let's go.'

As they walked into the mess, the cook was washing up.

'Can you rustle up some grub, Cookie?'

'I've chicken and chips or chicken and chips or, at a push, a cheese sandwich.'

'Chicken and chips please and the same for you, Corporal?'

'Yes, please.'

'Two, please.'

'Are you that new SAS sergeant?' the cook asked with a grin.

'I'm afraid if I tell you I would have to kill you.'

Once they got their meal they went to the Burco Boiler and made a mug of coffee each.

'That's the Sergeants' area,' the Corporal said as James went to sit down.

'Fuck that, Corporal, you sit with me and we can talk. I don't want to shout.'

'But the Major is a stickler for the rules.'

'Sit down and that's an order.'

'Yes, Sergeant.'

'Pity he hasn't got anything better to do.'

'Colonel Wiseman wants to see you at 0930 in the morning.'

'Zero nine thirty hours, right.'

Once they had chatted for a while James got up. 'I think that's it for tonight. I've things to do. Thanks for the information. I'll see you around. Good night, Corporal.'

'Good night, Sergeant.'

James found his way back to his room, put his gear away, then got into bed and lay there thinking of Candy and her bed. He would much rather be there than here lying on more bumps than you would get sleeping on a bag of potatoes. All the same he was soon asleep.

At 0630 hours James was awake. He got out of bed and stretched, then he got his washing kit, picked up his weapon and went to the ablutions. Another soldier came in.

'What's the water like?' he asked.

'Wet and warm.'

'That's normal. I've not seen you before. I'm Sergeant Walker.'

'Sergeant MacDonald.'

'Pleased to meet you. You're the SAS sergeant brought in for training, right?'

'You're right.' The jungle drums had been beating already. They all knew why he was here, or so they thought. They both finished washing.

'Are you going for breakfast'? Sergeant Walker asked.

'Yes.'

'Well, if you like I'll come with you.'

'Fine, I'll finish dressing and meet you here in five.'

'See you in five.'

In the canteen it reminded him of the services – the trays on the hot plate laid out close together and side by side. The first tray had fried eggs, then sausages, then bacon, tomatoes, beans, black pudding, fried bread and – a surprise – chips. They helped themselves to two of each and a few chips, then took their trays over to the sergeants' area.

James noticed that the eyes of most of the soldiers eating were on him. They were talking in low voices. He was the new boy and they didn't know what to expect.

At 0930 he was outside the Colonel's office.

'You can go straight in, Sergeant.'

James entered the office and stood to attention.

The Colonel said, 'Stand easy, and take a seat, Sergeant.'

'Why haven't you got a beret on, Sergeant?' asked Major Franklin.

'I didn't bring one with me, Sir. Can I get one from the stores with your cap badge on it? Mine would stick out like a sore thumb.' *What an arsehole!*

'He has a point, Major,' the Colonel replied. 'The section you'll be training is Corporal Brown's section, the section that came out for you last night.'

'That's fine, Sir. Can I ask what routine Captain Burke had?'

'Yes, he did training Monday to Thursday. Friday and the weekend he set work for the section and then did his own job.'

'Can we stick to the same routine, Sir?'

'Yes, of course.'

'Do you have any unmarked cars and can I use one of them at the weekends?'

'Major Franklin will arrange that and tie it up with the Motor Transport, Sergeant.'

'Anything else, Sergeant?'

'Yes, Sir, have you got any false number plates?'

'I don't think so. Have we, Major?'

'I don't know, Sir, but why would we need them?'

'When I go out, even though it's the same car, an assortment of different number plates can confuse anyone watching the vehicles leaving the barracks.'

'You think of everything, Sergeant.'

'I try to, Sir; that's why I'm still around.'

'I'll get the Major to see if we've any false number plates. Corporal Brown will get a beret for you and he will escort you to meet his section.'

'Thank you, Sir, shall I wait in the outer office?'

'Yes, please.'

In the outer office James sat in a chair thinking of nicknames for his new superiors. 'The Colonel I would nickname "Owl" because he's a Wiseman, the Major I would call "The File" because he's a right old bastard.'

A short while later Corporal Brown took James over to a classroom which was a Portakabin, with little more than a few chairs and a blackboard, a piece of chalk and a cloth duster.

'This is Sergeant MacDonald. He will be in charge of all the training for this section from now on.'

'Relax, lads! I don't bite … well, not very often, but you'll find that when it comes to training I'll be hard but fair. I have to earn your respect and you've to earn mine. Anything in the training you don't understand you ask for it to be done again and again until you do understand. A section is like a lion with two heads, the Corporal and the Lance Corporal, but the rest are just as essential. Now, when I point to you, I want you to give me your rank and name. Let's start with the two heads.'

James started to point and each one stood up and answered.

'Corporal Peter Brown, section commander.'

'Lance Corporal Ben Minter, second-in-command.'

'Pte Phil Edwards.'

'Pte Larry Hart.'

'Pte Bruce Small.'

'Pte Ian Cady.'

'Pte John Baker.'

'Pte Len Bird.'

'Pte Greg Smith.'

'Pte Alan Cage.'

'For the Corporal and Lance Corporal we'll just use their

rank. Pte Phil Edwards will be Pip. Pte Larry Hart will be Lamb. Pte Bruce Small will be Tiny. Pte Ian Cady will be Caddie. Pte John Baker will be Doughy. Pte Greg Smith will be Smithy. Pte Alan Cage will be Jailbird, and Pte Len Bird will be Dickie. Now that you've your nicknames remember them! This will help me put a face to them, so that if we go into action and I can't remember your name, as soon as I say your nickname you'll know who I mean.'

'The Major would go spare if he knew, Sergeant,' the Corporal said.

'Well, let's hope he doesn't find out, but I bet you a week's wages that he calls everyone of non-rank just Private.'

'You're right, Sergeant.'

'What time do you have dinner, Corporal?'

'If we're in the barracks training, normally 1200 hours, Sergeant.'

James looked at his watch. It was fifteen minutes to.

'Dismiss them for dinner, Corporal. Back here at 1300 hours.'

'Yes, Sergeant.'

At 1300 hours they were all back sitting in their chairs ears pricked ready to see what was going to happen. They had been laughing and joking while they were at dinner, mainly about their nicknames.

'Patrols – what are they used for? Tiny, can you give me the answer?'

'To see where the enemy are, Sergeant.'

'That's only a small part of it. Mainly it's to deny the enemy use of the ground.'

'Who heads the patrol and who is the tail-end Charlie? Lamb?'

'The Corporal takes the lead and Doughy is normally the tail-end Charlie.'

'The Corporal is in charge of the section but *anyone* can lead and *anyone* can be the tail-end Charlie.'

'But we've not been trained to do those jobs,' said Jailbird.

'Aye, but you will. With your method your poor Corporal and Doughy must be dead on their feet and that's the time when mistakes are made and they can be fatal. If everyone can do the job you spread the workload amongst you all. Remember, you are a team. Corporal, when is your next patrol?'

'Tomorrow night at 2200 hours, Sergeant.'

'Do you know the route and area?'

'Same as the last time. It's always the same.'

'Who plans the route?'

'The Major. It's marked on a map which we collect from the office, Sergeant.'

'When will you collect it?'

'Tomorrow morning, Sergeant.'

'As soon as you get it, bring it to me.'

'Yes, Sergeant.'

'Look, lads, anything that I say in this room stays in this room. It's my job to keep you alive and give you the best training that I can give you. I say to you: do not use the same route every time you go out. It's not a walk in the park and you've every chance of getting ambushed.'

'Will you change the route, Sergeant?' asked Tiny.

'Too fucking right I will. Fridays, Saturdays and Sundays I have to work elsewhere but tomorrow I shall be on patrol with you.'

'With *us*, Sergeant?' Caddie asked.

'Yes that's my world out there. Lance Corporal, while your corporal is with me and we're planning the patrol, I want you to get the section together and clean and oil all weapons and check all working parts. Also check all your equipment.'

'Yes, Sergeant.'

'Corporal, when you've collected the map we'll have a briefing here, so let me know when.'

'Yes, Sergeant.'

'Carry on, Corporal.'

*   *   *

On Friday morning James was having breakfast when Corporal Brown walked in.

'I've got it, Sergeant,' he said, waving the map at him.

'Good, have you had breakfast?'

'Not yet, Sergeant.'

'Have your breakfast and I'll meet you at the cabin and bring your lance corporal with you.'

'Yes, Sergeant.'

After breakfast he made his way to the cabin. Ten minutes later the corporals arrived and the map was laid out on the table.

'It's the same route as we did three days ago on our last patrol.'

'Do you know what section was in this area last night?'

'No, Sergeant, but I can find out from the office.'

'We'll find out and see if you can get the section commander of that patrol to come and see me.'

Corporal Brown left the cabin. While he was gone, James and the lance corporal worked their way around the route – it was 90 per cent on roads.

'Did you stay on the roads?'

'Yes, Sergeant, we keep to the exact route as marked.'

Corporal Brown walked in with another corporal.

'This is Corporal Clark of Two Section.'

'Thank you for sparing the time to come and see me. What I would like you to do is take a look this map and tell me if this is the route you took on your patrol?'

He studied the map and then folded it up and looked at the back.

'That's the map I took out. See, I made a note on the back of the map, a map reference.'

'Did you stick mainly to the roads?'

'Yes, but we did cut one corner to catch up a bit of time. Was that all right?'

'Fine. Thanks for your help, Corporal.'

As soon as Clark had gone, James turned to Corporal Brown. 'Corporal, will you see if you can get me a map that hasn't been marked, a map case and a chinagraph pencil.'

'Yes, Sergeant, I'll not be long.'

'Lance Corporal, see if you can get three coffees, please. Mine's black no milk or sugar and the other two the way you and the Corporal like it.'

'Yes, Sergeant.'

When they came back James folded the map and put it in the case so that Keady was in the centre of the case. Armagh, Keady, Market Hill and Newry were all showing through the plastic of the map case.

'This is the new route. Same area as you can see, but we're mainly off the main roads and also using the best cover we can find. Your comments, please, gentlemen.'

'I agree with you, Sergeant, but the Major will throw a wobbler.'

'If you lads want to live, then we do it my way. Let him throw a wobbler, as you put it. How many men have you lost while on patrols?'

'Five in the last two months and that's when we started our tour of duty, Sergeant.'

'I rest my case. Get the section to have dinner and get their heads down and we'll meet back here at 2130 hours all kitted up and ready to go.'

'Yes, Sergeant.'

At 2120 hours the section was in the cabin and James walked up to each member of the section and checked them out. When he got to Tiny he asked, 'Have you got the call signs?'

'Yes, Sergeant, we're alpha one four and Headquarters is alpha two zero.'

'And the section in the next area?'

'Bravo one four, Sergeant.'

'Are your water bottles all full with fresh water?'

'Yes, Sergeant,' they all replied.

'Corporal, move them out.'

They formed up outside and, as they moved out through the gate and headed for Market Hill, James gave the order to cock the weapons and put the safety catch on. At Market Hill they skirted around the town and followed the route cross country towards Newtownhamilton. As they passed a farm gate a bullet hit the gate and lodged in one of the gate rails right close to Doughy Baker.

'Down!'

James ran to the gatepost and lay beside Doughy.

'That was fucking close, Sergeant.'

'Take your helmet off and put it on the muzzle end and, when I say, raise it so it is just above the hedge.'

James pushed the safety catch off.

'Now!'

Doughy pushed the helmet just above hedge. Two short bursts sprayed about a metre either side of the muzzle flash.

'The bastard shot my helmet!'

'Which one, Doughy?'

'I'm lying on one, thank God.'

'Stay down. Keep your eyes peeled.'

Doughy was looking through the gate.

'Sergeant, there looks like two bodies lying out there. Shall I take a look?'

'Don't move and don't touch the fucking gate. Tiny, radio in contact and wait out; that's all.'

'Pip, you're the nearest to that hedge and you've got cover all the way. Check him out but be careful.'

'Yes, Sergeant.'

He was away, crawling on his belly close to the hedgerow towards what he hoped would be a dead body. The rest of the section just lay where they were, keeping their eyes peeled as they waited for Pip to get back. Half an hour later Pip returned.

'I've not seen shooting like that, Sergeant, He's dead as a dodo. Bullet between the eyes. I've marked the spot with white tape.'

'Well done. Corporal on me.'

Corporal Brown came over and James got his adapted torch out and switched it on. He looked at the hinge side first – clear – then the opening side. There was an explosive taped to the post, and a pin with a piece of thread tied to it with the other end pinned to the gate so that when the gate was opened it pulled the pin out and good night, Dick.

'Doughy, do you still want to go through the gate?'

'No, I've already been hit in the helmet. I don't want my balls blown off as well.'

'Corporal, hold that pin in tight.'

'Yes, Sergeant.'

'Stop shaking. Just do it.'

James pulled the Velcro on his trouser leg and pulled out one of his knives and cut the string. He also cut the tape and removed the bomb from the gatepost. The tape that was left hanging on the bomb he wrapped around the pin so that it held it in place. James opened the gate.

'Cover me.'

He went forward. The two bodies were lying side by side with their arms outstretched to form a cross. They were naked and they had been cut from just below the Adam's apple to just above the penis and from nipple to nipple across the chest. They had been shot in the back of the head and by the lack of blood in the vicinity they had been killed somewhere else and then dumped here.

'Tiny, radio in and tell them to get in touch with the Royal Ulster Constabulary to collect three bodies and give us an estimated time of arrival. We'll wait and hand over to them.

Corporal, give Tiny the map reference. While we wait, we'll take up defensive positions.'

Tiny was busy on the radio talking to HQ. After he had finished he said, 'The RUC will be here just after first light.'

Corporal Brown lay on the ground next to James.

'May I ask you some questions, Sergeant?'

'Yes but you might not get answers to all of them.'

'How did you know there was only one man out there?'

'If there had been more than one they would have fired together. Does it make sense – two men two targets?'

'How did you know where he was?'

'I knew that when Doughy put the helmet up if he took the bait I would see the muzzle flash, so I aimed at the muzzle flash and allowed a metre either side. Two short bursts usually do the trick because most will wait to see where their bullet hits. When the bullet hit the helmet he was dead.'

'How did you know that the gate was booby-trapped?'

'I didn't know the gate was booby-trapped, I just guessed. Why leave two bodies that can be seen from the road? Because they wanted them to be seen and the gate to be used.'

'There's a lot to being a soldier. I thought it would be easy but there's a lot to learn.'

'Don't let it worry you. You'll make a good soldier and you've a good section and trained right they will make you proud of them. But just one thing: welcome to my world.'

'Sergeant.' It was Tiny. 'When we get in the Colonel wants to see you in his office with Major Franklin.'

'I bet he does.'

'Will you be in trouble, Sergeant?'

'We shall see. How many rules have I broken since I've been here? More than a fistful.'

'Can we help, Sergeant?'

'Yes, if asked, tell them exactly what happened and what I've done except for the next bit.'

'What is the next bit then?'

'The men who killed those men might have left tracks, so we're going to be Indians and do some tracking.'

The RUC turned up and an inspector walked over. James stood to attention and saluted.

'Sergeant James MacDonald, Sir.'

'Inspector Collins.'

'I'm surprised, Sir, to see you. You would never get our top brass out of the barrack gates without a tank.'

James explained everything that had happened and that he had not touched the bodies just in case they were booby-trapped. He gave him the bomb that he had taken from the gate.

'Thank you, Sergeant, you've done an excellent job and it could have saved some of my officers' lives.'

'By the way, Sir, there's a body along that hedge over there.'

'What did he die of?'

'Lead poison – I shot him.'

'Some shooting, Sergeant.'

'Thank you. Could you do me a favour? Could you ring Colonel Wiseman and thank him for what his men have done. It could just save my career, Sir.'

'I'll ring as soon as I get back.'

James headed the patrol and walked in a semicircle around the bodies until he had picked up the tracks in the grass. He called up Corporal Brown.

'Can you see where the grass has been flattened with the weight of a man. It shows up as a slightly lighter colour.'

'It's hard to follow but I can just make it out.'

'It's going in that direction across the field.'

They followed the tracks across the field to the gate on the opposite of the field to where the bodies lay. He checked the gate just in case there was another surprise. It was clear, so they went through the gate and on to a road. They crossed over and he sent the corporal down the edge of road looking for tracks, while he went in the other direction doing the same. After about forty metres, in the grass in front of another farm gate, there were tyre tracks. Another set of tracks went towards the farmhouse.

'Corporal, they had a car waiting here, so there is no more we can follow, so take over your patrol and get them back to the barracks.'

'Yes, Sergeant.'

Back at the barracks James knocked on the Colonel's door. The major and the colonel were both present, and both looked less than happy.

'Sergeant MacDonald reporting, Sir.'

'Sergeant MacDonald, Major Franklin tells me you changed the orders for the patrol last night, and I want to know why?'

'I didn't change the orders. I just changed the route. We were still in the area that was to be patrolled , Colonel.'

'Why did you change the route, Sergeant; it was all marked out on the map?' shouted Major Franklin.

'Do you want an honest answer because you won't like it?'

'What do you mean?'

'Did you give this map to Corporal Brown with the route marked on it in ink?'

'Yes, why?'

'Well, you gave the same map to Corporal Clark the night before. Here is where he wrote down a map reference, and in my book you do not send a patrol out on the same route every night because, if the patrol is being watched, the enemy knows exactly where it's going to be at any time throughout the night. Colonel, if you don't like the job I'm doing, may I suggest that you ring Major Tompsett to transfer me.'

The telephone rang and the Colonel was on the telephone

for a good ten minutes. He replaced the receiver and stood there rubbing his chin with his right hand.

'That was an Inspector Collins of the RUC thanking me for the way my men performed last night. He reckons that they saved some of his men's lives. The man you killed was a well-known sniper and was wanted for up to a dozen killings. That was some shot at that range, Sergeant. But let's get back to the matter in hand – the broken rules.'

'I don't break the rules just for the sake of it. If I had gone to the Major he wouldn't have changed a thing. In my view Corporal Brown should be using his knowledge of the area to work out a different route each night.'

The Colonel sighed. The Major just looked annoyed.

'Come back at 1630 hours and I'll decide what to do then.'

'Yes, Sir, may I make a suggestion that you ask Corporal Brown for a verbal report on what happened because I might be accused of bullshit. That section went out as boys and came back as soldiers. See you at 1630 hours, Sir.'

In the mess all the privates were in deep conversation about the events of the previous night. As soon as they saw James, you could have heard a pin drop.

As he walked past he nodded casually. 'All right, lads?'

'Yes, Sergeant,' they replied in unison.

Chapter 7

At 1630 hours James was sitting in the outer office waiting to see the Colonel.

'You can go in now, Sergeant.'

'Thank you.'

James walked into the office, stood to attention and saluted.

'Sit down, Sergeant. I've spoken to Corporal Brown and have listened to the full events of last night. I didn't believe it so I spoke to the rest of the section and Private Doughy Baker showed me the hole in his helmet.'

'The dirty bastard, Sir.'

'What's that supposed to mean?'

'Private Baker showing you the hole in his helmet.'

The Colonel looked puzzled. 'The whole barracks is talking about it, and the morale is the highest it has ever been. To them you're a hero.'

'I'm no hero. I'm a soldier, nothing else, and I try to do that job to the best of my ability.'

'Anyway, I've given it plenty of thought and from now on you'll report to me alone. Any changes you want to make we'll sit down and discuss them.'

'What does the Major think of that? I bet that has put his nose out of joint.'

'I don't care what the Major thinks. I'm in command of this unit and what I say goes.'

'Yes, Sir, but I would prefer that the Major was present when we discuss any changes; otherwise he's going to feel like a spare prick at a wedding and no one likes that.'

'I'm beginning to like you. When the Inspector congratulated you, you didn't take the praise for yourself or the SAS; you gave it to us.'

'They were your lads that were there. They did the work and under fire they handled themselves well and that's down to you, Sir. When I wear your cap badge, I work for you.'

'I spoke to Private Pip Edwards and he reckons the sniper you killed was shot in the head and died instantly.'

'Lucky shot, Sir. Can I use the secure line and have the unmarked car at 2100 hours, please?'

'Certainly, it's the red telephone on my desk. While you're on the telephone, I'll sort the car out.'

James rang the number he had been given, the receiver was lifted.

'Major Randall speaking.'

'Hello, Major. Sergeant MacDonald, code name Shadow.'

'What can I do for you?'

'Have you or any other regiment lost two men? Only last night while on patrol we found two bodies that had been cut open to form a cross then shot in the head. The RUC have the bodies, and I don't think they were just soldiers.'

'I'll have to check this out and come back to you later. Where can I reach you?'

'Armagh Barracks, on the secure line. Do you have the number?'

'Yes. I'll get back to you as soon as I've any information.'

'Thank you, Sir, and for your records a Sean MacBride was shot and killed last night. Do you know of him?'

'Yes he was one of their top snipers. We've been after him for years. He makes a hit and then scarpers across the border.'

'Well, last night he forgot to get a return ticket.'

The Major laughed. 'I'll be in touch as soon as I can and thank you, Sergeant.'

He put down the receiver and looked at the Colonel.

'You're a dark horse, Sergeant, I bet you never told the RUC that you thought they were soldiers?'

'No, Sir, I just handed them over. It's up to them to investigate and not for me to do their job.'

'Your car is laid on and when they ring back I'll send an orderly to fetch you.'

'Thank you, Sir.'

James saluted and left the office. He was stopped by the orderly.

'Major Franklin would like to see you in his office, Sergeant.'

'I wonder what he wants. If a phone call comes through for me, you know where I am.'

'Yes, Sergeant.'

'Thank you, Corporal.'

In the office Major Franklin was standing behind his desk.

'Thank you, Sergeant, for coming to see me. We may have got off on the wrong foot and I would like to say I'm sorry.'

'Accepted, Sir. May I say something without you going off half-cocked. It's about officers.'

'Yes, go on, Sergeant.'

'The trouble with officers is they sit on their arses, pushing papers and doing the administration, and I know it's got to be done but they never go out of the gate and come into my world. If they were to go out with one of their patrols, they would gain a lot of respect from their men and they would know what the men face every time they go through the barrack gate and on to the streets. I'm not taking the piss out of you. Your world is here; mine is out there. But when officers make rules that tie one hand behind your back, well, it makes me mad. With respect you could be the first one to change all that.'

'Give me a chance to think about what you've said. Can I ask: have you ever been offered a commission?'

'Yes, but I turned it down for all the reasons I've just told you about. Could you see me sitting in an office?'

'To be honest, no.'

'You know that the Colonel wants me to report to him.'

'Yes, I've been informed.'

'Well, I've asked the Colonel for you to be there as well and get involved in the decisions made. I'm not trying to undermine your authority. I want to work with you and stop your men getting killed or at least give them a fighting chance.'

'Thank you, Sergeant, I respect your frankness.'

James shook his hand and left the office to go back to his room.

The orderly shouted at his back, 'Telephone, Sergeant.'

'Thanks.'

He walked back across the yard and into the Colonel's office.

'Telephone, Sergeant.'

'Thank you, Sir.'

James picked up the red telephone.

'Hello.'

'Hello, Major Randall here.'

'That was quick, Sir.'

'You were right, Sergeant. A mailman and his backup are way overdue for reporting in. Although I can't confirm it, I would say you're right.'

'Thank you, Major, can you do me one more favour? On your files or through your informants, could you find out if there's a IRA cell working over here or on the mainland with a man in it who smokes a Dutch brand of cigars called Meharis. I know it's not much to go on but it's important.'

'That's a tall order but I'll see what I can do.'

'Thank you, Sir, goodbye.'

'Goodbye.'

James went back to his room, changed into his black

Gortex suit, strapped the knives into position and pulled on a pair of baggy jeans over the top. He then put on a three-quarter-length coat and a pair of black trainers and then packed two black plastic bags, two bottles of water, two cheese sandwiches, two chocolate bars, one of the Walthers and half of the ammunition in a small black holdall. The other Walther and the rest of the ammunition went into the coat pocket. James checked to make sure that the knives were in the right position and that the Velcro undid easy. All ready to go, he grabbed his bag and went down to the Motor Pool. Waiting for him was the Motor Transport Sergeant.

'The car's all ready. It's the dark-blue Ford. It's not in the best of condition body-wise but it's fast and goes like shit off a shovel. Here are the keys. It's all tanked up and ready to go.'

'Thanks, Sergeant.'

'You must be mad or a very brave man. You wouldn't get me out there for all the tea in China. We send a patrol just to get the newspapers and that's just across the road.'

James laughed. 'Did the Colonel ask for some spare false number plates?'

'Yes, I've six pairs.'

'Could you make sure that when I have the car you rotate the number plates, please.'

'Will do! Good luck and bring her back safe and sound. I've got attached to the old girl.'

'I'll do my best.'

James went out through the gate and took the road to Portadown. He kept checking in his mirrors. He couldn't see any car headlights but that didn't always mean that you weren't being followed. Time to do a bit of backtracking: at the next roundabout he went all the way around and doubled back the way he had come. He put his foot down and the car accelerated with great speed. He eased back on the throttle, smiling at the car's performance. He then turned into the road that ran by the farm where the patrol had tracked the men to last night. About a third of a mile down the road was a wood. He found a track which he could drive down with care. He eased the car along it as he didn't want to do any damage to the underneath of the car like knocking off the exhaust pipe or damaging the sump and losing all the oil.

He managed to find a place to turn the car around so he was facing the way he had come in, just in case he needed to make a quick getaway. That *would* fuck up the bottom of the car.

He got out of the car and closed the car door quietly. He grabbed the holdall then locked the car. He stood looking and listening and waiting for his eyes to become accustomed to the dark.

He began to creep through the wood and from time to time would stop, look and listen. At the edge of the wood he stopped and looked through the apple orchard that lay between him and the farmhouse. The branches were being bent down with the weight of the fruit; it looked as if they were in for a bumper crop. He elected to crawl along the hedgerow that formed the boundary of the orchard.

At the edge of the orchard another hedge joined on and carried on past the side of the farmhouse. Where the two hedges met formed a T-junction. He found a place where he could see both the farmhouse and the yard. James pulled on the Velcro and pulled out a knife and made short work of cutting the twigs away and making a hole big enough for him to crawl inside the hedge. He cleared the ground of any item that would be uncomfortable for him to lie on, then he tied the twigs together to form a bung to block the hole once he was inside. He then tied a piece of green-coloured cord to the bung with which he could pull the bung back into place.

James settled down for a long night. Thank god it wasn't raining. Just a bit of a chill in the air. There was nothing worse than being cold and being wet right through to the skin. The farmhouse was an old ramshackle kind of a place with small windows. There were lights on in four of the ground-floor rooms. The upstairs was in darkness. There were three security lights, two on the house and one on the barn, so that the yard was bathed in light. Not good at all. Not far from the house and to the left there were two barns, the one with the light and one without. The barn without the light had no doors and James could see that there were two tractors and a lot of farm machinery. The other barn had new doors and big hasp and staple secured by a massive padlock.

Why padlock one barn and not have doors on the other one when it has a tidy few grands-worth of machinery in it? He sure would like to know what was in there.

He was feeling drowsy when the unexpected happened. The door of the farmhouse opened and a bald-headed man stepped out, putting on a flat cloth cap. He was wearing brown corduroy trousers, a thick jumper and a brown-coloured jerkin over the top. He went over to the barn, undid the padlock and went inside, leaving the padlock hanging on its hasp but pulling the door closed after him

James strained his ears. He could just make out the hum of a small electric drill. He looked at his watch. It was 2345 hours. Funny time to be working! His eyes went back to the farmhouse. Everything was the same. He kept an eye on the windows that had lights at them. He hadn't seen anybody pass the windows so he was 80 per cent sure that the house was empty and he was on his own.

Eighty per cent! Not bad odds. Time to go. He pushed the bung out, reversed out of the bush with his holdall and replaced the bung and crept down towards the farmhouse until he was near to the area that was covered by the lights. As soon as he reached the yard he sprinted over to the farmhouse door, opened it quietly and stepped inside. He stood still to let his heart rate slow and listened for any noise that would let him know if he had company. All the internal doors were open so he picked the door on the left. He found himself in the kitchen with a big old oak table and an old cooking range. There were pots and pans piled in the sink and plates, cups, mugs, knives and forks all over the table. *Dirty old sod!*

James went into the living room. It smelt of stale tobacco smoke. It had a cabinet in one corner with photographs of a younger woman that could have been his wife taken a few years ago or even his daughter. A half-full bottle of Irish whiskey stood on the coffee table and there was a shabby three-piece suite. He had seen enough. Time to go to work. He hunted around the living room and then he found it in the hall – the switch to the security lights. They were on a timer. He twisted it and the lights went out. He slipped out through the door and, keeping close to the house wall, crept towards the barn.

At the barn door he listened and could hear the hum of the electric drill. He put his left hand on the door, opened the Velcro and pulled out a knife from its scabbard. He pushed the door open and slid through the gap and pushed the door closed. Whether it was the noise, change of temperature or even instinct, the farmer put his hand on to a post to twist himself around to face James but too late – the knife was already on its way towards its target. It went right through the man's right hand, pinning it to the post. He screamed out in pain and looked at James who already had the other knife out ready.

'Stand still or you'll cut your bloody hand off.'

'Who are you and what do you want?'

'I'm the one who's asking the questions. Now stand still and I'll take the knife out before it does any more damage. See what a nice gentleman I am.' James moved in close and kneed the man in the bollocks before pulling the knife out at the same time. The farmer dropped to his knees moaning and groaning. James saw some black tape on the bench. He grabbed it and taped his wrists together. He also picked up a dirty old rag and wrapped it around the damaged hand.

'It's a bit dirty but you won't die of gangrene. I don't want you to bleed to death before you've answered a few questions, do I?'

'Bastard!'

'Now you can have it hard or easy; it's up to you.'

'Go to hell!'

'I'll bet you'll be there before I am. Fancy the odds? Now to business. Last night with three other men you killed two soldiers and left them in a field not far from here. Who were you with?'

'I'm not saying.'

'Wrong answer. Same question.'

'Same answer.'

'Don't be a hero because you'll be a dead one.' James picked up a shovel and hit him in the knee with the back of the shovel blade.

'You bastard!' the man screamed between clenched teeth.

'I'll give you a bit of time to think about it. If you can take it, I can dish it out and you've not seen nothing yet. Are you going to answer the question.'

There was no reply.

James swung the shovel and hit the damaged hand. The pain must have been excruciating.

'Talk or am I wasting my time?'

James lifted the shovel again.

'No more, no more! I can't take any more.'

'Talk!'

'All right, all right. Conner Murphy, Head Hill Farm, Keady. Jerry Wilson, The Wood Yard, Portadown Road, Markethill. Terry O'Shea, 40 Armagh Road, Newry.'

He hit him again. 'Have you told me the truth?'

'Yes, yes!'

'Who's the top man?'

'I don't know, honest.'

James scribbled the names and addresses down and put them in his pocket. He then found a length of rope and tied the man to the post, then looked around the workshop. There were three made-up bombs on the bench with pins in just like the one he had cut off the gatepost. He put two in the holdall, picked up the shovel and went over to some animal pens. He started moving the hay. There was nothing until he got to the middle pen, then the jackpot: underneath the hay were wooden planks covering a pit. He pulled up four planks and exposed what was in the pit – an arms cache. Rifles, pistols, machine pistols, ammunition, Semtex and one machine gun. It was Christmas and his birthday all at the same time. He climbed into the pit and retrieved two UZI machine pistols, four magazines and boxes of ammunition. He put them in an old sack and stood it by the door ready to take with him.

In the workshop he found an old fishing rod with a reel attached. He took the reel off the rod then cut the fishing hooks off the line and tied it to the pin on the bomb that he had left on the bench. The man watched him with gathering fear in his eyes. James taped the bomb to the post, grabbed his holdall and his sack of goodies, and ran the fishing line out as far as it would go. He pulled the line, the pin came out and the bomb exploded.

James got up and ran through the orchard. He could hear more explosions. The hay must have caught fire and set off the Semtex and ammunition. He kept running till he reached the wood. He slowed the pace and worked his way back to the car.

On Sunday morning it was 1000 hours when he was awakened by a knock on the door. James sat up in bed.

'Come in.'

86

Corporal Brown walked in.

'Have you heard, Sergeant?'

'Heard what?'

'You know the farm where we found those tracks?'

'Yes, well?'

'A man was killed there tonight and the RUC were crawling all over the place. He was a bomb maker and he blew himself up it seems. There was a quantity of arms and ammunitions there, too.'

'How did you know about it, Corporal? Were you there?'

'I don't know what you said to the Major but he gave me a map and said plan your own route and we came down through that farm.'

'It's getting better all the time.'

'Sorry to bother you, Sergeant, but I thought you should know.'

'No that's all right. I do like to know what's going on, Corporal. Thank you very much.'

The Corporal closed the door behind him and James fell back into a deep sleep.

Chapter 8

Monday morning at 0800 James was already in the cabin, when the section walked in and sat down. The atmosphere was electric.

'Good morning, lads.'

'Good morning, Sergeant.'

'Have you seen the papers, Sergeant?' asked Corporal Brown.

'No I only read the obituary column and that's to see if I'm still alive and kicking.'

Brown lifted the paper. '"Bomb maker blows himself up on a lonely farm near Keady".'

'Wasn't very good at his job if he blew himself up.' James turned to a tray covered with a cloth.

'Gentlemen, there are pencils and paper on the tables. Make sure you've one of each. On this tray there are twenty-four items. You'll have thirty seconds to look at them and remember what they are. Then twenty minutes later you'll have two minutes to write down as many as you can remember.'

At that moment the door opened and the orderly walked in.

'Sorry to bother you, Sergeant; the Colonel wants to see you in his office as soon as possible.'

'Tell the Colonel I'll be there.'

'Yes, Sergeant.'

'Corporal Brown, take over, you know what they have to do and don't let them cheat.'

'They won't cheat, Sergeant; you can be sure of that.'

James put on his beret on and went over to the Colonel's office, he went in and stood to attention and saluted.

'Good morning, Sir.'

'Good morning, Sergeant. Major Randall wants to speak to you. You can give him a call, red phone.'

He picked up the telephone and dialled the number.

'Major Randall?'

'Yes, speaking.'

'Sergeant MacDonald, Sir. You wanted to speak to me?'

'Yes I've a problem and was hoping that you could help. Yesterday the Ulster Defence Regiment were ambushed on the road to Portadown, an officer was killed and a young woman corporal was taken hostage. The IRA have demanded the release of an activist who was captured last week and they have given us twenty-four hours or she will be killed. I've spoken to your Commanding Officer, Colonel Hickly, and he has refused to help, saying that he is over-committed, but suggested that you might be able to help.'

James smiled. His CO wanted to get rid of him one way or another. 'How many men have you got who could deal with a hostage situation?'

'None. As you know my men are used for surveillance and gathering intelligence; they would be no good for this job and would probably get her killed.'

'We need a four-man team, Sir. For one man it would be like committing suicide, and you want me to take it on?'

'Yes. I know by the way that you killed the bomb maker the other night even if the RUC don't. If you can do that, you'd stand a chance with this problem, even if it's a slim one.'

'That's blackmail! How did you know that I was even there, let alone that I killed him?'

'My job is intelligence, Sergeant.'

'All right, hands in the air ... Do you even know where she's being held?'

'Not at the moment but we're working on that and should have the answer later today.'

'Tell me all you know about the captive right to the last detail. I want to know how she will react.'

'Her name is Kate Fareway. She's a corporal in the Ulster Defence Regiment and has three years' service; she's not married and has no children; she has auburn hair and green eyes, is five foot five inches tall and weighs about nine stone and is a really good-looking woman. We think she would have difficulty in handling the situation.'

'You'll have to talk to Colonel Wiseman as you know I'm working for him but if he agrees I'll have a go. But I need as much information as you can get hold of and I'll also need a driver who knows the area as I can't leave an unmarked car sitting around. We can work that out later. I'll pass you over to Colonel Wiseman.'

Colonel Wiseman took the phone and was talking to Major Randall for a good twenty minutes. He put the telephone down and turned to James.

'Sergeant, that's a diabolical situation. What sort of chance do you think you have?'

'Little or no chance, but it all depends on how good they are and what security they have.'

Colonel Wiseman was sitting at his desk scratching his head and looking worried. 'I'll wash my hands of this one and leave it up to you, but without you she has no chance.'

'You know I was going to do it anyway but I need your help with teargas, stun grenades, a gas mask, ammunition and a few other items. I'll make a list.'

'Anything you want. I'll give you all the help I can. Did you know you've been here only five days and I've aged ten years.'

'You don't look too bad for your age, Sir. I'll see you later when we've more intelligence.'

James left the office and went back to the cabin.

'Have you finished?'

'Yes, Sergeant, here are the papers. They're not brilliant – the highest was eighteen, the lowest ...'

James interrupted.

'We don't want to know who has the lowest score; it's an exercise I want you to do when you're hanging around the barracks. The idea is to improve your power to remember what you see and recall it later; it's used in sniper training but we can use it for reporting incidents.'

'Have you done sniper training, Sergeant?' asked Jailbird.

'What do you think?'

'The way you were shooting the other night I would say that you have.'

'You've answered your own question.'

'Will we have sniper training?'

'If you are interested there are courses available, but it would have to wait until after your tour of duty. Now I want you to imagine a landscape picture on the wall of a country view, with hedgerows, roads, streams, houses, and perhaps hills and valleys. Now in your mind divide the picture up into three equal parts horizontally; the top third is the distance, the centre part is the middle distance and the bottom third is the foreground. When surveying the area, start at one side of the foreground and survey it until you get to the other side, then move up to the middle ground and survey back to the other side, then up to the distance, surveying back to the other side. Always start at the foreground because this is closer to you and therefore more of a threat.'

James looked at his watch. It was 1230 hours and not one of them had mentioned dinner.

'Now after dinner, when you get back I want you to get another piece of paper, write your names on the top and write a report on all that happened the other night when I was on patrol with you. Now you can have dinner.'

It wasn't long before James was talking to Major Randall again.

91

'Sergeant, we've got the location where she's being held. It's in a factory unit on an industrial estate just outside Portadown.'

'Where did this information come from, Major?'

'From an informant. He has always been reliable and the information cost me enough.'

'You wait till you get my bill. I ask questions because my life is on the line here.'

'I understand but when can you go, Sergeant?'

'I need the car and a driver here at 1700 hours and I need a three-quarter length coat like the ones farmers wear; a large one, too – there's a lot of equipment to conceal. Tell your driver if any more information comes to light.'

'Will do. Thank you and good luck.'

'I'll need a lot more than luck. I need a bloody miracle.'

At 1700 hours a white beaten-up Ford Fiesta with go-faster strips down each side drew up in the compound. Talk about a getaway car; the only things it could outrun would be a milk float or a bicycle. The driver got out and introduced himself.

'Hello, Sergeant, I'm Corporal Carmody. I've a coat and a cloth cap for you.'

This gets better and better, James thought. *Should have been Corporal Comedy with a bloody car like that.*

They left the barracks. The corporal knew his job; he was keeping to the speed limits, though that was easy in this rust bucket. He kept checking his mirrors just to see if they were being followed; he also took a few back roads just to make sure.

'This is the industrial estate. It's number 22; it should be down here on the right.'

'Corporal, can you do a slow drive by and then park about two hundred metres past the unit?'

'Yes, Sergeant, no sweat.'

The units were old with wooden sliding doors with

numbers painted on them. The sliding doors had small doors in them so you could get in and out without having to open the big ones. James noted the old metal fire escapes that went up to the second floor. On the other side of the road there was two empty units not being used. Corporal Carmody stopped the car another one hundred metres past the empty units.

'What time do you want me to pick you up, Sergeant, and where shall I park?'

'I don't know. Just how long it's going to take. You can't risk staying in one place or even keep driving around. If we're lucky, we'll make it back on our own.'

'Rather you than me, Sergeant. Good luck.'

'Thanks. I'm going to need it.'

James got out of the car and picked up his holdall and started to walk down the road. He crossed over and stopped beside the alley that led to the back of the disused units. He slipped down the side of the building to the back. Each unit had a small yard that had a wooden fence around it and a small road ran behind the yard the whole length of the buildings, then turned just past the last unit to join the main road that led into the estate.

Most of the windows had been smashed by kids.

James climbed the fence and dropped into the yard and stayed still, looking and listening to see if he had been spotted. All was quiet. He went to one of the broken windows, took his gloves from the holdall and carefully removed the broken glass from the windowsill. He put his hand inside and tried the catch. It opened and he climbed in. The ground floor was empty, just a concrete floor. To the left there were a couple of rooms; he opened the first one which had two toilet cubicles and a urinal.

The other room had a sink and a cupboard with a worktop. He went over to the window and looked out. It overlooked the alley which he had used to get to the back. He opened the window and then closed it but left the catch undone.

A staircase led up to the second floor. He climbed the stairs and went into the main office at the front of the unit. He stayed back away from the windows but could see out – the glass was intact because it was at the front and overlooking the main road.

At the rear of the unit there were three smaller offices with broken glass all over the floor; he didn't bother to go in. In between the rear offices and the front office was a room with no windows. It just had a wide bench that was fitted to one wall and some empty boxes littered about and the door was still on its hinges and still worked.

Back in the front office James settled down and took a pair of binoculars off his belt and watched the unit he was told the hostage was being held in. There was no movement that he could see. He kept watching and about an hour later the door opened and a man came out of the small door and walked down the road towards the main road to Portadown. He stayed there and kept watching. After twenty minutes the man returned carrying a carrier bag. He opened the door and walked in. James checked his watch; he had probably gone to get food. Being September it was beginning to get dark; the street lights came on, although they were not very good and only some of them were working.

The lights were turned on in the unit, but he wondered how many were in there. James knew he had to get closer to find out. He looked at his watch. Twenty forty-five hours. It was time to move. He picked up the holdall and climbed out though the window and dropped into the alley. He pushed the window to and keeping to the side made his way to the front of the building. He peered up and down the road. There was no movement so he ran across the road and down the side of the unit to the road at the back. Keeping to the shadows he worked his way to the unit he wanted.

He went to the fire escape and climbed to the landing. The door was locked and had bars across the glass panel. There was a window that was next to the door but it was about thirty inches from the end of the landing. There were no bars and the fanlight was open but it would be very difficult to get to. James stepped out, put his foot on the windowsill and grabbed the top of the window. He reached his arm in through the fanlight and undid the window. He stepped back on to the handrail and back down on the landing, picked up the holdall and then climbed through the window and on to a mezzanine floor.

There was a lot of small machinery about. A staircase led down to the ground floor. The mezzanine floor covered three-quarters of the unit and there was a tubular handrail across the front of it. He crawled slowly to the edge, undid the holdall, took out the two stun grenades and put them in his pocket. He also took out the Uzi and the spare magazine.

He peered over the edge. In one corner there was an office with glass in the top half. There were three men. One was about twenty, slim with dark greasy hair; the second man was about fifty-five, heavily built with grey receding hair and rotting teeth; the third man was in his forties, medium build and with a scar on his right cheek. Corporal Kate Fareway was naked and tied to a chair. Her hands were tied to the back of the chair and her legs were tied to the front legs of the chair. Her hair was a mess and she had a blindfold on. She wasn't gagged but was probably too frightened to make a sound.

One of the men was having a go at her. 'Only another twenty-four hours, then the deadline is up and then you'll be dead but before you die we may as well all have our way with you.'

He then got hold of her breasts and then pinched the nipples. Her body was shaking and she was sobbing very quietly.

'I reckon we ought to play cards for her, to see who goes first,' said the young one.

'Do you think you could handle it, boy? You don't look as if you've a good fuck in you.'

Slowly James crept down the stairs with the holdall. Close to the office wall near the doorway, he stopped and waited. He watched as the young one got a pack of cards out of the desk drawer and placed them on the table.

'Highest card wins?'

'I like the sound of that. Come on, cut,' said the man with the scar.

'I've a jack,' said the young one.

'I've an eight,' said Scarface.

'I've a four,' said the old one.

'I've an ace so I've won the Queen,' James said as he stepped through the doorway and opened up with the Uzi. The young one was dead before he hit the floor. Old Scarface had his throat torn away – he tried to stand up but a burst in the chest put paid to that. The middle-aged man was shot in the head and fell to the floor.

James put his hand over Kate's mouth, cut the ropes and took off the blindfold. She was free.

'Don't scream. We've still got to get out of here, all right.'

She nodded. He cut the shoes off the young one and gave them to Kate.

'Put them on!'

'My clothes.'

'They're not here. Now go.'

James grabbed her hand and forced her to the back fire exit and pushed the bar. As the door opened a bullet hit the door frame alongside his head. He turned around. A man had just come in through the front door. James didn't bother to aim. He just raked the area until the magazine was empty, then grabbed Kate and together they ran up the service road, turned left alongside one of the units and across the road to the open window. James lifted her up and pushed her through then followed her in, pulling the window shut behind. Again he grabbed her hand and ran upstairs to the storeroom. He took out a knife and cut the cardboard so it lay flat on the bench, picked her up and sat her on the cardboard. He undid his jacket.

'Open your legs!'

'No, no, no!'

'Don't be silly. We've got to get you warmed up or you could die from the cold.'

He stood between her legs and pulled the jacket around her and pulled her close to him, then started to rub the back of the jacket to cause friction and get a certain amount of heat into her. She turned her head and laid her face against his chest.

'Hello, Corporal Kate Fareway. Let me introduce myself – Sergeant James MacDonald SAS at your service.'

'Thank you for what you've done.'

'Relax! Calm down! I've never tried this position before.' He laughed.

She shuddered.

'Did they do anything to you?'

'Their hands were all over me. They pushed their fingers inside me.' She began to cry.

'Come on, don't cry.' He kissed her forehead. She held on tight, gently sobbing in his arms.

James took off the jacket and got her to put it on and then he did up the buttons and the belt. He then lifted her back on the bench and grabbed the holdall.

'Are you hungry? Did they feed you?'

'No they didn't feed me. They said it was a waste of money as I was going to die.'

'Well, you're not going to die. Here, have a chicken sandwich and a bottle of water.'

'Thanks, you do know how to treat a lady.'

James smiled. He could hear police cars and people shouting. He went to the front office. It was all going on – flashing lights, police rushing to and fro.

'We've got to get out of here? Do you know this area?'

'Yes, down this road is a council estate and up the road is the main Portadown Road.'

'Can you bypass this bit and get out through the council estate to get away.'

'Yes.'

'Come on, let's go. When we get out of the window we'll go down the service road at the back. Put your arm around me as if we're lovers just on our way home.'

At the estate James looked at his watch. It was 2330 hours. He picked a car and smashed the small side window and opened the door and got in. Then he smashed the steering lock and hotwired the ignition. He opened the passenger door and Kate jumped in.

'Direct me to Armagh Barracks.'

They parked the car in a lay-by near to the barracks, wiped off any fingerprints that Kate had left, and walked up to the gate. They were challenged by the guard.

'Sergeant James MacDonald and another. Write it in the book.'

'It's all right. I've seen you around the barracks, Sergeant.'

He let them in and they went straight to his room.

'Go on, get into bed.'

She handed him the jacket and got into his bed.

James took off his shirt, jeans, trainers and knives and jumped into bed.

'Don't be afraid but I think we both deserve a cuddle.'

She laid her head on his chest and was quietly sobbing.

'Come on, you're safe now. In the morning I'll get you some clothes from the stores then we'll ring Major Randall and have you picked up.'

'Did you kill those men who held me captive?'

'No, I just beat them at cards.'

Kate pushed herself against him and he stroked her face. Soon she fell asleep.

In the morning James slid out of bed and got dressed and went to the stores and saw the Colour Sergeant.

'Can I have a set of combats to fit a person about five foot five inches tall and the smallest pair of boots you've got.'

'I know the Colonel told me to give you what you want, but what do you need these for?'

'It will all become clear later on in the day but for now it's my little secret.'

'I can't wait to find out. Here you go. Sign here.'

'Thanks, Colour.'

'No bother. I'm just intrigued.'

He went back to his room and gently woke Kate and handed her the combats and boots. She got out of bed and put them on.

'You look quite sexy in those but I prefer you naked.'

He grabbed his wash kit and they went to the ablutions and, while Kate had a shower, he stood outside the cubicle door. He handed her back her combats then took her back to his room, then left her there while he had a shower. When he returned she was brushing her hair; she looked a picture. They headed for the Colonel's office. The orderly looked up with his mouth wide open.

'Sergeant MacDonald to see the Colonel.'

The orderly picked up the phone. 'Sergeant MacDonald to see you, Sir.'

'Send him in.'

'The Colonel said go in.'

'Thank you, Corporal.'

James went in, stood to attention and saluted.

'Colonel, I would like to introduce you to Corporal Kate Fareway. Corporal Fareway, Colonel Wiseman.'

The Colonel looked at Kate standing there with her auburn hair.

'It's a pleasure to see you're safe and sound. You look good in one of our uniforms.'

'It's nice of you to say so, Sir.'

'How did you manage to get her out, Sergeant?'

'Long story, Sir. Let's say I won her in a card game.'

James smiled at Kate and she smiled back.

'What time did you get in last night?'

'About 0100, Sir.'

'Where did you sleep?'

'My room, Sir, I don't mind sleeping with lower ranks.'

Kate was laughing.

'He was a perfect gentleman, Sir. I had nothing to be afraid of.'

'I'm glad to hear it.'

'Colonel, could you ring Major Randall and ask him to pick up Corporal Kate Fareway this afternoon because I'm taking her to dinner first if that's all right, Sir. It's worth losing a stripe for.' A big smile came across his face.

'You remind me of me a few years ago.' The Colonel went over to the telephone and rang the number. They listened as he outlined the situation to the Major. The latter was clearly pleased. Eventually the Colonel put the receiver down.

'You could get another medal for this, Sergeant.'

'When they ask for your recommendation ask if I can have the money instead.'

'Anyway, they'll be here to collect you at 1500 hours, Corporal.'

'Yes, Sir.'

James and Kate left the office and walked over to the mess.

'Kate, what will you do now – stay in the Army and carry on or will you leave?'

'Stay in I think. I'm a lot stronger person now than I was, I wouldn't mind being taken hostage again if you were to come and rescue me.'

'No! You're too much bloody trouble. The first time you took the clothes off my back.'

'Only your jacket!'

'Well, why did you stop there?'

'You know why.' She looked at him a bit straight.

'I know. I was only joking. It was too bloody cold in any case.'

'You pig!'

'How did you get caught?'

'We were on a routine trip to Portadown when we came across what looked like an accident. Sergeant Greene stopped and got out of the Land-Rover. He was shot. Do you know how he is?'

'Kate, he didn't make it. I'm sorry but I had to tell you the truth.'

Tears filled her eyes and he reached across the table and held her hands tight.

'Thank you for being honest.'

'Can you carry on talking?'

'Yes, I had a gun shoved in my face and I was forced into the back of one of the cars. Well, you know the rest really.' Tears filled her eyes again. 'The trouble is I know that I'll have to answer questions and that worries me.'

'Ask to make a written report and no questions.'

'Thanks, James, I don't know what I would have done without you. You've been so kind.'

'Forget it! Now what would you like for dinner?'

He got up and went over to the hotplate and looked at what was on offer. 'Roast beef, roast pork, roast chicken, cottage pie and for vegetables they have roast potatoes, mash potatoes, carrots, peas and cabbage.'

'Have they got Yorkshire puddings?'

'Yes.'

'I'll have roast beef, Yorkshire pudding and vegetables and gravy, please.'

Cookie came over to the hotplate.

'I'll get that for you, Sergeant. Where did you find her? She's a bit tasty.'

'Picked her up in my travels. You can take it over to her if you like.'

'Can I?'

'Yes and maybe she would like another cup of coffee.'

Cookie took her dinner over and chatted to her. Then he went and made coffee and took it over to the table. James had finished dishing up his own dinner and went back to the table and sat down and looked at Kate.

'If I looked like you, do you think that I would get my dinner brought over?'

'Of course you would.'

She was laughing again and that was good.

'Where do you live, Kate?'

'Just outside of Loughgall with my family. Maybe you could come for a meal sometime?'

'No way! I would put you and your family at risk, an Englishman visiting an Irish girl.'

After dinner they went outside and strolled around the yard. At 1500 they went into the outer office.

'Top brass is in with the Colonel, Sergeant, but they said that when you turned up to go straight in.'

'Thank you, Corporal.'

He knocked on the door and walked in with Kate. He stood to attention and she stood to attention beside him.

'Sergeant MacDonald reporting, Sir.'

'This is Colonel Kelly, Commanding Officer of the Ulster Defence Regiment Loughgall, and Major Randall.'

James shook their hands. 'I'm pleased to meet you, Sir.'

'I would like to thank you personally for what you've achieved in getting the Corporal out of the clutches of the

IRA. Well done, Sergeant. Can you tell us what happened and how you managed it?'

James turned and looked straight at Colonel Wiseman. 'Can the Corporal wait in the outer office please, Sir?'

'Yes, Sergeant, that will be fine.'

James opened the door to the outer office and said to the orderly.

'Can you look after the Corporal for a while, please?'

'Yes, Sergeant.'

'It may seem strange, Sir,' he said as soon as the door was closed, 'but I want to spare Corporal Kate Fareway's feelings. You'll see why.' James quickly outlined the events of the previous night. They listened in awe. 'Can I ask you a favour, Sir,' James said at last.

'Yes, what is it.'

'Don't ask her any questions. Let her give you a written report in her own time. She's had a tough time.'

'That's no favour, Sergeant, that's common sense. I can see what a good job you've done to keep her positive, because we thought she would be a shaking wreck.'

'She also wants to carry on as a soldier, which surprised me a bit because I thought she would quit.'

'Can I have a written report, Sergeant?'

'I'm sorry, Sir, I don't write reports. I've told you what happened and you'll have the Corporal's report. Without disrespect, Sir, officers push pens. I'm a soldier and fight, that's why I was asked to do the job.'

'I admire the way you stand up for yourself, Sergeant. Therefore no report required.'

'Thank you, Sir.'

James went to the door.

'Will you come in, Corporal.'

Corporal Kate Fareway walked in looking a bit sheepish. She stood to attention.

'Are you really all right, Corporal.'

'Yes, Sir, I'm fine.'

'Sergeant MacDonald has asked me not to question you about your ordeal, but to let you write a report in your own time, and I agree with him.'

'Thank you, Sir.'

'That will be all, Sergeant.'

'Yes, Sir.' James saluted and walked out of the office followed by Major Randall.

Outside the Major spoke to James.

'Just a word, Sergeant. Well done! You did a brilliant job but where did you get the Uzi from?'

'Uzi, Sir?'

'Yes, Uzi.'

'The bomb maker gave it to me and then went to pieces.' James winked and the Major looked puzzled for a moment then laughed a little nervously. He turned to Kate.

'Come with me, Corporal. It's time you went back to your family.'

Chapter 9

The following day the Colonel asked James to come to his office. He got straight down to business.

'Major Franklin has informed me that he wants to go on patrol with you tomorrow night. What's the idea behind that. I assume, Sergeant, it was *your* idea?'

'The men see him as a wimp with no bottle, but he's not. If they see him out there with them it won't only boost moral but it will give the Major more confidence in his own ability.'

'What happens if he gets killed?'

'Then he didn't learn quickly enough, Sir, and you'd have to replace him.'

'You're a hard bastard, Sergeant.'

'I've had to be to survive. You went to Sandhurst, Sir, and learned to be a gentleman and a man manager, platoon and battalion tactics, how to write and file reports and to be one of the top brass. This is why I don't do reports. I was trained to be an animal, kill at the drop of a hat in any way that I can. I live on my wits and experience. My world is entirely different from yours, Sir, but I still wake up some nights sweating and seeing the faces of the men I've killed, especially those I took out with a knife. You can see the fear in their eyes and they die still pleading to be spared.'

In the cabin Corporal Brown and the rest of the section were busy doing the memory test. When James walked in they looked up with big grins on their faces.

'How come you get all the good-looking crumpet, Sergeant, and we don't get any?' asked Doughy Baker.

'Have you looked in the mirror? You're just bloody ugly and I've seen the state of your helmet.'

Every one was laughing, even Doughy.

'Is it true what we've heard – that she was taken captive by the IRA, Sergeant, and you had to go out and rescue her?'

'Yes, she was too good to leave with those bastards. You must agree with me on that score?'

'Too true. She was a real good looker, Sergeant.'

'Sergeant, I've picked up the map for the patrol. Tonight's patrol of Newry. Do you want to do the route?'

'No, Corporal, that's your job. You've done it before. Work your own route out, arrange for a driver, three-toner and an escort for the driver. Pick a drop-off point and tell him you'll radio in with the time and location of the pickup point.'

'Yes, Sergeant.'

'This is an urban patrol on the streets which is far more dangerous than a country area. The enemy are a lot closer to you and there's more cover, so keep your eyes sharp and, if we stop, use doorways, walls, corners of buildings, alleys and even cars. And now I've a surprise for you, and no it's not a bit of crumpet each. You've an extra man on patrol tonight besides me. Major Franklin is coming along. Put him at number five; I'll take six.'

'Yes, Sergeant.'

There was a lot of muttering going on.

'Give him a chance like you did me and make sure you all get some sleep before we leave. Carry on, Corporal.'

'Yes, Sergeant.'

At 2100 hours the section was back in the cabin working in pairs checking each other's equipment to make sure that they had not forgotten anything and that webbing was done up tight. Corporal Brown was checking with Tiny to make sure of the call signs. Major Franklin turned up and the Corporal saluted.

'Welcome to the section, Sir. May I have your permission to check your equipment?'

'Yes, Corporal, you have my permission.'

'Thank you. Sir. All right.'

They all went outside and got into the back of the three-toner. Even the Major got into the back. The escort came round to do the tailgate up.

'Have you got a round up the spout, Private?' James asked.

'No, Sergeant, not allowed.'

'Well, you are allowed now, so please cock the weapon and put the safety catch on and tell the driver to do the same and when you get back use the unloading bay.'

'Yes, Sergeant.'

Corporal Brown gave the order for everyone to get in, then the truck pulled out of the gateway and headed for Newry. As they reached the outskirts the truck slowed and came to a stop. They debussed quickly and the truck went back. The corporal formed his section ready to move off, with the Major at five and James at six, and off they moved. The streets were quiet with hardly anybody about and they carried on with the patrol.

The patrol turned into a road of small terraced houses.

As they were walking down the road, James noticed that one house had an upstairs window open. It was the bottom window and it was one of the old type with a sliding sash. Now it was September, not warm enough to require a window open and, even if it were, why push the bottom up and not the top down? Then a hand came out through the open window with a 9-mm pistol pointing at the patrol.

James pushed his safety catch off and fired a burst in through the open window. There was a scream. He had hit his target but nonetheless he saw the finger tighten and pull the trigger. The round slammed into the bonnet of a parked car, then the pistol fell out of the sniper's hand and landed on the road below.

'Pip, back me up.'

James ran towards the door and fired a burst at the lock on the door. Still running he hit the door with his shoulder and the door flew open with an almighty bang. One step and he was standing at the bottom of the stairs looking up.

'Fuck me, that fucking hurt.'

Pip was standing covering the other two doors. James shouted up the stairs.

'Throw your fucking weapons out and then follow them out with your hands raised. No tricks or it will be your last.'

'All right, all right! I dropped the pistol, my arm hurts.'

'Come out, hands on head!' James screamed.

A woman in her late forties came through one of the other doors and started shouting.

'What are you doing in my house? My children are upstairs! Get out of my house! You people cause nothing but trouble.'

'Shut up!' he shouted. He put a foot on the bottom of the stairs. 'Now are you coming out or do I have to come up and fucking get you? You'll be leaving in a body bag if I do. Your choice.'

The sniper stepped out on to the landing, one hand on his head, the other hanging limp by his side. He was very young.

'Don't shoot, don't shoot!'

'You're lucky I don't blow your fucking head off. Now get down here.' He addressed Pip. 'Call up the nearest man.'

'It's the Major, Sergeant.'

'Well, get him to spread him in the road face down and search him for any weapons. Then keep him covered. Now is there anyone else up there? I want the truth now.'

'No, no.'

James kicked him in the groin as he went past.

'Lying bastard! Come on, throw your weapon out and then follow them out, hands on head.'

No one answered. James fired a burst up the stairs and the bullets smashed into the wall.

'Give me a grenade, Pip. That will make him come out.'

Pip looked at James dumbfounded.

'I'm coming out.'

There was a clatter on the landing as another pistol was thrown on to the landing.

'Come out, hands on head!'

A man of about thirty came out hands on his head.

'Now slowly come down the stairs.'

He did as he was told and Pip took him outside and got him to lie down on the ground alongside his mate. The woman was still blubbering and shouting.

'My baby, my baby, what have you done to him?'

'I shot the bastard and if he had stuck his head out of the window I would have decapitated him. Is there anyone else upstairs?'

'No, no, honest to God.'

'May I get someone to have a look?'

'Yes, but please may I go to my boy?'

'Are they clean?'

'Yes, Sergeant.'

'Go on but don't do anything silly or he could still die of a complaint called lead poisoning when I shoot him. Lamb, check out upstairs but be careful. Tiny, what state is the radio in?'

'Contact and wait out, Sergeant.'

'Clear, Sergeant.'

Lamb passed James and returned to take up his position. James walked over to the younger one.

'Name?'

'Gerry Forbes.'

'Well, Gerry, you made three mistakes tonight. One,

you're a boy playing with men's toys. Two, you don't stick your arm out of a window, you fire from *inside* the room, and three, you don't fuck with The Shadow when he's in a mood.'

Then he went up to the other guy.

'Name?'

No answer so he stood on his hand.

'Sorry, name?'

'Patrick Bonner.'

'Tiny, get on the radio and get them to get the RUC to collect the rubbish and radio back an ETA.'

'Yes, Sergeant.'

Lamb came over with the pistol which he had picked up by the barrel from the landing.

'Well done! Keep hold of it. Has the other one been picked up?'

'Not yet, Sergeant.'

'Go and find it, Lamb, and treat the same as you did this one.'

'Yes, Sergeant.'

The mother was stroking the boy's head.

'Why did you try something like this?' she sobbed. 'It will never do any of us any good at all.'

'I wanted Dad be proud of me.'

'What will happen to him?' the woman said, addressing James.

'Twenty years plus for attempted murder. Pip, use your field dressing and stop the flow of blood.'

'The RUC will be here in twenty minutes, Sergeant.'

'Thanks, Pip.'

'Will you see if you can see where the bullet hit.'

James went over to the Major.

'Are you all right, Sir?'

'Yes, fine. Thank you, Sergeant.'

'When the RUC get here if they send an inspector will you

do the handing over? It will look a lot better for you to do it and your own men will appreciate it.'

'That's all right. Will do.'

'Thank you, Sir.'

The RUC inspector turned up. It was the same one who had come out the other night. He walked over to James.

'Hello, Sergeant, you make my job interesting and give me a lot more work. Trouble must follow you around. What happened here, can you tell me?

'The Major will hand over and tell you, Sir.'

'Where the devil did he park his tank?'

'You had better ask him, Sir.'

'I certainly will.'

'It's Major Franklin, Sir.'

'Thank you, Sergeant.'

'He hasn't got one with him, Sir.'

The Inspector looked astonished and James watched with interest as he walked over to the Major. The Major looked as if he was in control, even a little bit proud of himself. A few minutes later the Inspector came back.

'You're no ordinary soldier. Twice I've seen your expertise with a rifle and I also think that a certain bomb maker was down to you. If you ever want a job come and see me. I'll give you one.'

'Sorry, Sir, the colour of the uniform doesn't suit me.'

The Inspector laughed. 'Well if you ever need any help and want a cleansing service, give me a call. I'll fax my special phone number through.'

'Thank you, Sir, I appreciate that.'

The Inspector was still laughing as he walked away.

Back at the barracks they debussed and went to the unloading bay. Then they went to the cabin and sat down. James got two chairs, one for the Major and one for himself.

'Corporal Brown,' James began, 'Once again I have to congratulate you and your section on the way you conducted yourselves tonight. You're all professional soldiers and I'm proud to be associated with you. Now are there any questions?'

'Yes, Sergeant, how did you know that we were going to be hit at that time and place?'

'Always look for the things that are wrong. A window open in September, for instance … Any more?'

'Yes, Sergeant, I would like to ask one.'

'Go ahead, Major.'

'Why did the Inspector ask me where I had parked my tank?'

'Well, I'll be honest. The first night we were on patrol and we called the RUC in and the Inspector asked where the officer was. I said you wouldn't come out of the barracks without a tank, but you proved us wrong.'

Corporal Brown was more of a diplomat. 'Not a question, Sergeant. I would just like to say that it's all down to you the way you train us and the way you perform. Nothing frightens you and we would follow you anywhere. And just one other thing: we would like to thank the Major for coming out on patrol. Three cheers for the Major.'

'Hip hip … hooray!'

'Hip hip … hooray!'

'Hip hip … hooray!'

'Major, I'd like to say something, too,' James added.

'Yes, Sergeant.'

'Major, welcome to my world!'

James stood up and shook the Major's hand.

At 1000 hours James was back in the cabin. The section arrived.

'Good morning, lads. Before we start on training is there any comment on last night's patrol or any questions that you've thought of?'

'Yes, this is the first time when on patrol that we've ever

captured anyone. Do we have to be so hard on them?' asked Pip.

'My answer to that is, yes, you want to keep them on their toes and let them know that you are the boss and hold all the aces. Then he's not going to try anything silly ... Yes?'

'Why do we call the RUC in when we have a contact.'

'They're the law and it's down to them who can prosecute them. Are there any more questions?'

No one answered.

'Now let's move on. Setting up roadblocks ...'

At the end of the morning session James kept Brown behind. 'Corporal Brown, would you stop back, please? I'd like to speak to you.'

'Yes, Sergeant?'

'Would you be prepared to drive the unmarked car later and drop me off in Newry? I would like to be there at 1700 hours. I'll arrange for you to drive the unmarked car. As soon as you've dropped me off, only do a few back-doubles and keep to the speed limit unless you run into trouble. If you run into a RUC or UDR roadblock, give them my name and ask them to get in touch with Inspector Collins if it's the RUC and, if it's the UDR, it's Major Randall 14 Intelligence at Loughgall. Have you got that?'

'Yes, Sergeant. How about picking you up?'

'I'll find my own way back, but thanks for thinking of me. I'll go over to the office to sort things out. Oh, and Corporal, you'll need a pistol.'

James walked over to the outer office. As ever the orderly was sitting behind his desk.

'Hello, Corporal, is the CO in?'

'No, Sergeant.'

'How about the Major?'

'Yes, I'll tell him you're here.'

'Thanks.'

'You can go in now, Sergeant.'

'Thank you.'

James walked into the office, stood to attention and saluted.

'Can I ask a favour, Sir?'

'Yes, Sergeant.'

'I would like to use the unmarked car at 1615 and for Corporal Brown to drive it and drop me off in Newry and then return here with the car. As the Colonel's not in, if the Colour Sergeant rings, can you give him confirmation for the issue of a 9-mm pistol and three mags of ammo, Sir.'

'Going for a ride in the country?'

'I'm just going to see an old mate. He will be pleased to see me, I know he will.'

'I bet he will.'

'Did Inspector Collins fax through his special telephone number? He said he was going to.'

'I don't know to be honest, but you could check with the orderly.'

'If he has got it, can I use the red phone, please?'

'No problem.'

'Thank you, Sir.'

James stood to attention and saluted and retired to the outer office.

'Corporal, has a fax come through from the RUC from Inspector Collins?'

'Yes, Sergeant, it came through early this morning. It's on the Colonel's desk.'

'Could you go in and make a note of the telephone number for me, please?'

'Yes, I'll do it now.'

'Thank you, Corporal.'

James put the number in his top pocket, then went to his room and packed his holdall. One of the IEDs he'd taken from the bomb maker, his gloves and balaclava, the two

Walthers and four magazines. He also threw in about half a dozen plastic cable ties.

James changed into his jeans and a black sweatshirt, then he strapped the knives into position and checked they were in the right place. He did one final check and then he went to the MT shed.

Corporal Brown was already there waiting in the car. James put his bag down in the floor well.

'Did you manage to get the pistol all right?'

'Yes, but I had to check with the Major first because the Colonel wasn't in. He issued one.'

'Where is it?'

'In my waistband.'

'Try to pull it out.'

Brown had to lift himself out of his seat so that he could straighten his body enough to pull the pistol out.

'Put it under your seat on the floor so you can get at it quickly.'

'Where do you carry yours, Sergeant?'

'I've got one in my waistband, which is fine when you are standing, but I also have one in the bag between my feet.'

Corporal Brown started the car and pulled out of the gates and headed for Newry.

'Keep your eyes on the rear-view mirror and check that we've not got a tail. When we get to the next roundabout go around again and make it look as if you've missed the turning.'

'Sergeant, do you reckon I could join the SAS?'

'If you want an honest opinion, I would say, yes, have a go but leave it for two years and get more experience. You'll need to keep up the fitness training and when you get on the course remember they might hurt you but they won't kill you.'

'Where did you go for the induction course?'

'It takes place in Wales at the Brecon Beacons.'

They reached the outskirts of Newry and James was looking at the map on his lap.

'Just go another three-quarters of a mile. There's a church on the right. Drop me there.'

'Yes, Sergeant.'

Brown pulled up opposite the church and James picked up his bag and got out of the car.

'Get back and good luck.'

'You, too, Sergeant.'

Corporal Brown turned the car around and went back the way he came. James looked around. There were only a few people about, mainly kids playing football. On the corner of the next road there was a telephone box. Once he reached the box he stopped, had a good look around, then went inside and phoned the number the orderly had given him.

'Hello, Inspector Collins. It's Sergeant James MacDonald. I'm in Newry to see one of the bomb maker's friends. I want some information from him and I don't want to have to kill him, but I will if I have to. Can you get a search warrant for a house in Newry?'

'Yes, that's easy enough, can you give me the address?'

'I will when I've finished explaining. Once I've got the information I need I'll give you a ring and then you can go in and do your search. You'll find an IED which I borrowed from the bomb maker. How long will he get for possession of explosives with the intention of endangering life?'

'I should think the way the judges have been handing out sentences lately, probably ten to fifteen years. Why do you want to plant evidence? What has he done?'

'He was one of the men who killed the mailman and his backup. I could kill him but my reputation is growing too quickly. The Colonel even said he's aged ten years since I've been over here.'

'I understand why you want to slow down. I heard about the four at the factory unit in Portadown.'

116

'Well, can you be ready and as soon as I call move in I'll tell you where the IED is?'

'Yes, it will be a good catch but give me the name and address for the warrant.'

'Have you got pen and paper?'

'Yes, fire away.'

'Mr Terrence O'Shea, 40 Portadown Road, Newry. Have you got that?'

'Yes, I'll wait for your call.'

'Thanks.'

James came out of the phone box and walked towards the Portadown Road. The light was beginning to fade. He found a house with a number he could read – number 26, number 34 … He was going the right way then. He counted in twos until he reached number 40.

The front door was on the pathway. No garden. He didn't stop but kept on walking until he came to a crossroad. He walked down the road. As he suspected there was an alleyway that ran behind the houses, with a row of gates that led into the small back gardens.

The house on the corner was number 64. Number 40 then had to be the thirteenth house along. He came to number 40 and tried the gate. It was unlocked. He opened it and closed it again and walked on down the alley and back to the Portadown Road. He glanced at the house. It was still in darkness. No lights on in any room. He decided it would be safer to hide in the back garden, than roam the streets after dark.

So he walked around to the back gate, put on his gloves, opened the gate and wiped the latch. The garden was in darkness and, if he kept close to the fence and walls, he couldn't be seen. He tried the back door. It was locked with a Yale-type lock.

The windows were closed and they were the old-type wooden sash. He pushed on the window and it moved slightly in its frame. He pushed the top window tight against the top frame – this took the pressure off the catch – and then forced the knife blade between the two window frames and slid the catch over. He tried the window for ease of opening and also noise, then he left them in the closed position.

James waited in the darkness. At last the front door opened and a man and a woman walked in and turned the hall light on. They were noisy and laughing. They had been drinking and were two parts to the wind. They hung their coats up in the hall and came into the living room. They turned the light on, he said something to her, she turned the light out and they went upstairs.

James saw the light go on in the bathroom and then heard the flush being pulled. He waited a while then he pushed the bottom window up and climbed in. He went to the back door and unlocked it, putting the catch on to hold it in the unlocked position. He then closed the window; he had one bolthole out of the door if need be. In the holdall he found the IED and put it in the top drawer of an old writing desk. He pulled some papers over the top, took off his cloth cap and put his balaclava on. He took the Walther out of the bag and kept it in his hand, then went to the front door and did the same as he had done to the back door. He now had two boltholes.

At the bottom of the stairs he looked intently up the stairs. He could hear the bed protesting at what was going on. James crept up the stairs, keeping as close to the wall as possible so as to minimize any noise from a creaking staircase. He stepped on to the landing. The bedroom door was open. He took two plastic ties out of his bag. The bedroom light was out and the curtains were closed so there was no light coming in from outside. He could now see the up-and-down movement in the bed. Terry was getting near to the hurry-up bit at the end.

James turned the light on. 'Stay still! No noise and don't

either of you move or it will be your last. Lay still and put your hands behind your back.'

James put the cable ties on Terry and pulled them tight.

'And now roll off.'

Terry rolled off as he was told.

'Now, lady, no noise or you'll both be dead. Put your hands in front of you … Now sit on the end of the bed side by side and no tricks! I want a few answers to some questions.'

'Who the bloody hell are you?'

'Your worst nightmare. I choose if you live or die. Now sit at the end of the bed.'

'We've no clothes on!' the woman wailed.

'You don't need any to talk! Now move!'

They did as they were told. They were both in their fifties. He was heavily built, was bald on top but hairy as a gorilla everywhere else. She was of medium build with scraggy blonde hair and fairly large breasts that matched her hair – scraggy.

'Now your husband here has been a naughty boy. He and his mates killed two men the other night and dumped them in a field. It was gruesome stuff, too. Who were the men who were with you, Terry?'

'I didn't do it. I was here with my wife.'

'That's one lie. Any more and it will be the last. Your friend the bomb maker told me different. He gave me some names including yours, but went to pieces before we had finished talking. Now do you and your wife want to live?'

'You killed the bomb maker, didn't you? He was too good at his job to blow himself up.'

'Now I'll ask you one more time. What are the bloody names?'

'If I tell you'll you let us live?'

'Give me the right answers and you and your wife can finish your shag. If not, you'll still be stiff but very cold.'

'Tell him, Terry, tell him! I don't want to die.'

119

'Good advice, love.'

'All right. Conner Murphy and Jerry Wilson.'

'Who's the head man and who does he take orders from.'

'Jerry Wilson but I don't know where he gets the orders from. Honest, if I did know I would tell you.'

'Are there any more arms dumps around here besides the one at the bomb makers?'

'I can't tell you that. They would kill me if I tell you.'

'Well, I'll kill you if you don't. Your choice.'

'There are two of them. One in the tractor shed at Conner's place, and one in the wood near the wood yard.'

'Where exactly?'

'Go down the road past the wood yard, take the track to the left and two hundred metres along that track you'll come to a clearing. In the far corner, there's an old water tower. There's a pit underneath covered with timber and dirt put on top.'

'Now I'll let you live and you can finish your shag, but if you are telling porkies I'll be back and you won't like that. I hope you have an orgasm, love.'

He turned the light off and went out through the back door in the yard. He took the hood off and put his cloth cap back on. He went through the gate along the alley. When he reached the phone box he rang Inspector Collins.

'Hello, Inspector. Leave it about half an hour and then go into the living room. There is an IED in the top drawer of an old writing desk.'

'Well done! Speak to you soon.'

'Yes, Sir.'

He checked the map he had eighteen miles to tag, so it would take four hours to get back to barracks.

Chapter 10

At 0900 hours James was in the cabin. He tied a piece of cotton between two tables about two hundred and fifty millimetres off the ground to represent a tripwire attached to a bomb.

As he was going to the blackboard the section walked in.

'Don't walk down the centre aisle and take your seats. Good morning, lads. How are you? Is anyone missing?'

'No, we're all here, Sergeant.'

'Good, does any one know what the piece of cotton represents? Lance Corporal, what do you think it is?'

'I'd say a tripwire, Sergeant.'

'Well done, spot on. We've been on patrol but up to now we've not been on a track that runs through a wood, so today we're going to show you the right way to move along a track and how to check the track for tripwires.'

'Isn't it the same, Sarge, as a normal patrol spaced out on either side of the track?' Pip offered.

'Yes but the movement is different. Look.'

James went to the blackboard and drew two lines about one hundred and fifty millimetres apart. He then drew crosses on either side and just inside of the lines.

'These are the places for each man. First the section commander or whoever is leading the patrol. The second man would be four metres back but on the opposite side of the track. This carries on down to the tail-end Charlie. Now this is where it changes. At night the leader has a thin twig about one metre long and holds it out in front of him about

121

three hundred millimetres above his head. He brings it down slowly. What you are looking for is any resistance against the twig. If there isn't any you repeat the operation, only this time you start at your feet and move the twig forward and up. If the twig meets resistance, check if it's a tripwire. What would you do then? Pip?'

'Place a piece of white tape over it to mark where it is so you can see it on the way back.'

'I know that's what you've been taught but if I were the IRA then I would wait for you to pass, put another wire across the track about three metres away from the other one, adjust the wire and hang the marker over it. When you come back you step over the marked wire and straight into the trap. Can you see the sense of what I've said?'

'I would never have thought of that, Sergeant, but what should you do? Surely not just leave it there?' asked Corporal Brown.

'Now you're thinking! You get on your hands and knees and run your hand along the wire. The end will either go to the bomb or it will be tied to a tree as an anchor. If it's the anchor end, retrace the wire until you reach the bomb; if it's tied to the pin, then leave the pin in and cut the wire, put a piece of tape around the bomb and pin it so the pin can't be pulled out, and then take it with you. Then carry on with the twig if it's clear for the next five metres. The leader will kneel just in the wood on the opposite side from where he started. Once he kneels down and covers the track, then everyone moves across the track to the position the other man has vacated so you are zigzagging along the track.

'These tactics can also turn the tables on the enemy. If they start chasing you down the track the order would be "Ambush". The first two men stay where they are and the others move into the wood and then in to line. The first two take up fire positions and draw the enemy into the trap. Do you understand? When we do our next patrol Corporal Brown will give us a woodland track.'

'Sergeant, why have things changed to what we were taught a few months ago?' Doughy asked.

'Things change all the time. You have to keep learning.'

'What would you say our roll is over here?'

'It's more of a policing roll to keep law and order until a political solution is found, if ever. Corporal Brown, will you take over with the twig and the cotton? Blindfold them and make them practise so they can feel the resistance of the cotton against the twig.'

'Yes Sergeant.'

James walked over to the office and in he went.

'Is the Colonel in his office?' he asked the orderly.

'Yes, Sergeant. I'll ring through for you.'

'Thanks.'

'You can go in, Sergeant.'

The Colonel was on the phone so James waited until he had finished.

'Can you arrange for me to have the car tonight, Sir, at 0200 hours, please?'

'That's a funny time to want the car, Sergeant?'

'I know, Sir, but I want to be in place by 0300 hours.'

'I'll sort it out for you.'

'Thank you, Sir.'

'By the way, I've been talking to Inspector Collins and he told me to tell you everything went all right last night.'

'Did he say if Terry ever did get his leg over last night?'

'No, but why should he?'

'Well, I interrupted him in the middle of it, so I asked the Inspector to give him half an hour before he arrested him.'

'You're all heart, Sergeant, all heart.'

'I know, Sir, it's in my nature.'

'All sweetness and light.'

'Well, it could be his last shag for twenty years or more.'

123

'What did he do?'

'He killed the mailman.'

'Are you sure he's the one?'

'Yes but I'm not sure we'll be able to prove it so he was arrested for possession of explosives with intention to endanger life.'

'So they found a bomb or explosives on the premises?'

'Yes, I put it there and then told the Inspector where it was.'

The Colonel raised his eyebrows and was silent for a moment

'Is there anything else you would like, Sergeant?' he said at last.

'No, I think that's all, Sir.'

'I'll have the keys left in the ignition.'

'Thank you Sir, is that all?'

It was 0200 hours. Just before the wood yard on the right was a country pub with a big car park with only two cars parked up. James reversed alongside one and switched off the engine and lights. He would leave the car here; if anyone saw it they would probably think that the driver had too much to drink. He shut the door quietly and headed towards the wood yard. A sign pointed along a wide track: 'Jerry Wilson and Son, Timber Merchant'.

James moved along the track slowly, using the shadows and stopping frequently to look and listen. When he reached the clearing, he could make out the shape of the water tower, but instead of going straight across the clearing he skirted it until he was close to the water tower. He stopped and crawled to the edge of the clearing and looked and listened. Nothing. He moved to underneath the tower and felt the ground. It was fairly loose and not trampled down tight.

James left things as they were. He would get the RUC to raid it at a later date. He wanted information first. He took his bearings to where the wood yard was in relation to the water tower then crept through the wood until he was at the rear of the wood yard compound. It reminded him of a fort in the old Western films: logs had been fixed together to make an outer wall and at the front were two big gates big enough to take a lorry. The two centre uprights were chained together and locked with a massive padlock.

Inside the compound a big workshop was constructed in the same way as the outer wall but had a galvanized tin roof. He would have loved to be on the inside of the compound when Jerry turned up for work, but it would take too long to climb the compound wall and he would be compromised if any one turned up, so he decided against it. He would hide outside and see what happened and who turned up and what they were going to do.

James found a hiding place in the undergrowth where he could see the gates of the compound and also the wide track leading to the double gates. He also made sure that he had an escape route just in case he needed it. After a couple of hours there was movement on the track: a man was walking towards the wood yard. It was getting light. The man took out a bunch of keys and unlocked the gates and went inside. He was a young man in his early twenties, stocky build, wearing jeans, Dr Marten boots, a red-and-black checked jacket and a baseball cap. He was too young to be Jerry Wilson – could be his son or just someone who worked for him. After about half an hour he came out with a tractor and trailer which he had loaded with a petrol chainsaw, a spare can of petrol, ropes and chains and an axe. He stopped the tractor and closed the gates and relocked them, then he jumped onto the tractor and drove up the track deeper into the wood. Then he stopped and James could only just hear the idling engine, then nothing. The engine had been switched off and a chainsaw had started, so James knew whereabouts he was in the wood just by the noise.

Half an hour later a white transit truck with 'Wilson's Wood' in bold black letters on the side came up the track and stopped at the gates. The driver unlocked them and went inside. James stayed where he was, then he heard a machine in the workshop start up. He was working in the workshop but the young man could come back at any time so he would have to be the first target.

James crept up the track to where the noise was coming from. He saw the tractor first, crept up to it and then spotted his target cutting down trees. He skirted round so he could come in from the rear – with all the noise that the chainsaw made he didn't have much of a chance of hearing anything. James crept up behind him and gave him a heavy blow to the side of the neck. He went down as if he had been felled like one of his trees. James switched off the chainsaw and dragged him to the nearest tree, sat him against the tree, pulled his hands behind him and used the cable ties to handcuff him. He could stand up but to go anywhere he would have to take the tree with him. He went over to the tractor and took two pieces of rag, one he used as a blindfold, the other as a gag. He then took the keys from the young man's pocket. He was slowly coming to so James waited until he could understand what was being said to him.

'I'll be loosing the gag and I want some answers. No shouting or you'll die! Do you understand?'

He nodded and James took off the gag. 'I don't want to die.'

'Then do as you are told. Does Jerry drive a white transit van?'

'Yes.'

'Good lad, you'll live to a ripe old age. Now I'm going to re-gag you, so stay still.'

'All right.'

James put the gag back on and left him there. That was

126

one out of the way; now for the big fish. He went back down the track, back to the wood yard, and stopped at the gates. He looked and listened, then stepped inside. He undid the padlock that Jerry had locked in the chain and left hanging there. He closed the gates and wrapped the chain around and relocked it. He crept over to the workshop doors and peered around the door post. Jerry was using a planer to turn rough-sawn timber into planed timber and was stacking the result in a pile near his machine. There was a double-barrel shotgun leaning against a bench about two metres from where he was working. James pulled out the 9-mm Walther from his waistband and held it in his left hand. He stepped inside, picked up a lump of four-by-two and hit Gerry alongside of the ear. He was out like a light. James tied his hands in front of him and tied his legs together and lifted him on to a set of rollers that fed a massive circular saw which was used for cutting trees up into planks.

James put on his hood and waited for Jerry to come round.

'Hello, Jerry, does your head hurt?'

'Who the hell are you?'

'I'm getting fed up with that question. Everyone asks me that. Just say I was sent here by one of your friends to ask a few questions.'

'Who?'

'Your friend the bomb maker, a very brave man … at one time.'

'You killed him, you bastard.'

'If this was a quiz you would be well on your way to the jackpot. Now I'll ask you another. Who is the Englishman who gives you your orders and where can I find him?'

'*I* give the orders. They just do as they're told.'

'Bullshit!'

James started the machine and started to let him slide slowly towards it.

'Do you want your toenails cut? I'm good at chiropody.'

'Turn the fucking thing off. I don't know who he is. I've never seen him. Please turn it off.'

James flicked the switch and the blade started slowing down and then stopped.

'You'll have to do better than that. You may never have seen him but where can I find him?'

'My boy will be down for his break in a minute.'

'Sorry, he's sitting down on the job and if you don't answer me I'll go and have some fun with a chainsaw.'

'You bastard! Don't hurt my boy.'

'Talk then.'

James put his hand down towards the switch.

'All I know is there is an arms shipment being delivered to Four Oaks farm near Portadown next Thursday evening at nine and he will be there.'

'Are you sure?'

'Yes I'm sure.'

'How do you get your orders and use the information he gives you. Come on, talk.'

'I'm given a location and then pick up an envelope with the information inside and that's it.'

'Is that how you received the information about the mailman you and your friends killed?'

'Yes I had to go to a telephone box in Market Hill near the church. It was taped under the directory tray.'

'Is there anything else I should know?'

'No that's it; I've told you everything.'

'Did you know you are as thick as two short planks?'

James switched on the machine and walked away. He unlocked the gates, went out and then re-chained and locked them. He put his hood in the bag and threw the keys into the undergrowth. As he walked towards the car he heard Jerry's scream. He had never heard anything like it ever before.

James made his way back to the car. He checked underneath that all was right. Nothing. He unlocked the car and pulled the bonnet release catch, lifted the bonnet and looked inside. Everything was fine. He closed the bonnet, started the car and slowly pulled out on the main road and headed towards Armagh. Ahead was an RUC roadblock so he slowed down and opened the side window.

'Switch the engine off, please.'

James did as he was told.

'Where are you going?'

'Armagh Barracks.'

'Get out of the car and place your hands on the roof and stand with your legs apart.'

'What's wrong, officer? What's this all about?'

'Do as you are told.'

James got out of the car and placed his hands on the roof and stood with his legs apart.

'I'm Sergeant MacDonald, British Army.'

'Have you got any ID?'

'You know we don't carry any ID when we're working on a covert operation.'

One of the other officers was going through the car and picked up the bag. 'Look what I've found in this bag, Sergeant – a hood, plastic ties and a Walther 9-mm pistol and ammo.'

'I've told you who I am. Maybe you should check with Inspector Collins.'

James turned and faced the Sergeant, who punched him in the face and shouted, 'You don't tell me what to do. Put your hands on the car and don't move a muscle.'

He kicked his legs apart and they searched him and found the other Walther and ammo. They also found the two knives.

'Check with Inspector Collins and he will confirm who I am.'

'Look at these, boys. He thinks he's a proper Rambo. Cuff

him and put him in the back of the Land-Rover. Bill, you can drive the car back to Newry.'

'This is the third time: ring the Inspector.'

The Sergeant punched him again and split the eyebrow above the left eye.

'Keep your mouth shut and get in the Land-Rover or it will be the worst day of your life.'

The Land-Rover set off for Newry police station. The handcuffs started to cut into his wrists but he wasn't going to give them the satisfaction by complaining, so he gritted his teeth and took the pain.

They pulled into Newry police station and stopped as close to the door as possible. James was bundled into reception and they went straight to the desk. The desk sergeant was as thin as a rake, was losing his hair, and wore glasses that were perched on top of a long pointed nose. He looked more like a tax inspector than a police sergeant.

'What is he under arrest for, Sergeant?'

'Carrying weapons with intent to endanger life.'

'Can I've a list of his possessions?'

'One Walther 9-mm pistol, two mags of ammo, two knives in scabbards, one hood, one cloth cap and plastic cable ties.'

The desk sergeant wrote them on the charge sheet and said to James, 'Sign here.'

'I will when you put the right amount of gear down. There were *two* Walthers and four mags of ammo. Change it and I'll sign it. Leave it as it is and you can get stuffed.'

'Leave it! He will only be too happy to sign it later on. Take him to cell number 4.'

James was pushed along a corridor and bundled into the cell. It was about two and a half metres square. There was a toilet in one corner and a wooden bench with a blanket folded up on it. No pillows. Above the bench was a small window with bars. Just like the Hilton Hotel, a home from home. It was a wonder it didn't have a 'welcome home' mat on the floor.

James sat on the bench and waited. Two hours later two boys in blue came to the cell and took him to an interview room. The sergeant was sitting behind the desk. He reminded James of Bluto in the Popeye cartoons – thick beard and an ugly mug.

'Sit down.'

James sat down opposite him and the two officers stood behind him ready to wade in if he made a false move.

'Name?'

'I've already told you. Sergeant James MacDonald, British Army.'

'Bullshit! Name?'

'Donald Duck.'

'He's trying to be a comedian.'

He stood up and threw another punch. It connected and James was spitting blood.

'One day the boot will be on the other foot and you'll be sorry. I've got your card marked.'

'Take him back to the cell. We'll talk to him again in the morning. Maybe he'll talk then.'

James was taken back to the cell and locked in. He sat on the bench and wiped his eye with the back of his hand. He hadn't been given anything to eat or drink and he was starving. He tried to settle down and get some sleep, but it wasn't to be. It was about 0300 when he dropped off to sleep. He was awakened at 0600.

'Would you like tea or coffee?'

'Coffee please, black no sugar, and don't we get anything to eat in this place?'

'I only do the drinks.'

'What time does Inspector Collins get in?'

'This is not his station so I don't know.'

'Thanks anyway.'

When the coffee came, it was pushed through a trap in the door. It was cold but James drank it anyway; it was better than nothing. At 0900 a cheese sandwich was pushed through the door.

'Is this breakfast?'

'Yes, if you don't like it, complain to the chef.'

At 1100 hours bully boy and his mate came into the cell.

'Am I allowed a phone call or not because, if not, I'll have it put in the log?'

'Take him for his phone call and then when he's finished take him to Interview Room 3.'

James was taken into the reception area and led to a phone that was on the desk.

'Dial nine before the number you require.'

James picked up the phone and dialled the number.

'Hello, Inspector Collins speaking.'

'Hello, Sir, Sergeant MacDonald.'

'What can I do for you, Sergeant?'

'Come to Newry police station and ask for Sergeant MacDonald, Cell 4, Sir.' James replaced the receiver and was taken to Interview Room 3 and sat in a chair.

'Now, you runt, are you going to tell me your name?'

'I told you yesterday and I've not been christened again since then.'

'Trying to be the big man again, are we?'

'I don't have to prove anything and certainly not to you. You may be able to dish it out, but can you take it? One day you might find out.'

'What do you mean by that?'

'Just what I said. Some day I might be the one you won't want to meet in a dark alley.'

'Are you threatening me?'

'No, Sergeant, I don't make threats; I make promises and I keep them.'

'What were you doing in the area where you were picked up?'

'No comment.'

'Let's try again?'

'No comment?'

The door opened and in walked Inspector Collins. His face was white with rage. 'What the devil is going on here, Sergeant?'

'Just interviewing a prisoner, Sir.'

'And what happened to you, Sergeant MacDonald?'

'I just drove into one of your road blocks and met your sergeant here, so you had better ask him.'

'Well, Sir, we thought he was IRA. We asked for ID and ... and he said he ... he didn't have one because he was undercover.' The sergeant was beginning to stammer.

'What did he actually say?'

'He said that he was Sergeant MacDonald, British Army, and to check with Inspector Collins.'

'Then why didn't you get in touch with me. I'm only a phone call away and I would have told you to let him get on his way, but no, you've overstepped the mark this time.'

'Sorry, Sir.'

'You two go to reception and wait there for me. I'll be there when I've finished here.'

'I'm sorry, Sir. It won't happen again.'

'Bloody sure it won't. Now go!'

They left the room to go to reception and the Inspector turned to James.

'All I can say is that I'm sorry that this has happened to you, but what happened to your face?'

'Your Sergeant didn't like it so he thought he would rearrange it, but it was still no good.'

'I'll sort this out, I promise.'

'I'm far from happy and if that's how the RUC is run then I'll withdraw all cooperation and it will be up to the Colonel if he wants to cooperate. Because maybe he would like the glory when the two arms dumps I've found out about are hit. If I pick up my gear and it's not all there I'll go ballistic. I've been here for nearly twenty-four hours and all I've had is a cold cup of coffee and a cheese sandwich. May I leave now?'

'Let's talk about it.'

'No talk! Talk to the Colonel not me. I'll play it by the book and it's up to him what he decides. Now may I go?'

James got up and walked out to reception.

'I'll have my gear, please.'

The desk sergeant looked at the Inspector who was standing behind James.

'Give him his possessions, Sergeant.'

'Yes, Sir.'

As he put them onto the counter he ticked them off.

'Two knives in scabbards, one Walther and two mags of ammo, one hood and plastic cable ties.'

'Now you had better find the other Walther and two mags of ammo,' James shouted.

'That's all that's written in the book.'

The Inspector looked at the interviewing Sergeant. 'Where are the other pistol and two mags of ammo.'

'That's all there was, Sir. He must be trying to kid us and get another pistol.'

James moved like a tiger. He leapt at the sergeant and hit him straight between the eyes and he hit the floor like a sack of potatoes.

'Are the keys in the car? This is not over. If they're not returned to me I'll be back and I can assure you, you won't want me to come here again.

'Now you can see why there's going to be no cooperation from now on, so keep your men away from me. Otherwise I'll treat them as the enemy and when he wakes up tell him I made a promise and kept it.'

'Wait, Sergeant!' the Inspector pleaded.

But James kept on walking.

Chapter 11

As James pulled up to the gate the guard came over. 'Sergeant, the Colonel would like to see you in his office as soon as possible.'

James parked the car outside the MT shed, left the keys in the ignition, picked up his bag and went over to the Colonel's office.

'Sit down, Sergeant.'

James sat down and placed his bag on the floor beside the chair and looked at the Colonel.

'Inspector Collins has been on the phone explaining what had happened and apologizing. He said he has your missing items and will drop them in for you. They have also found a body at a wood yard and would like to know if you know anything about it?'

'Tell him it's up to him to find out who did it not me, and non-cooperation means just that.'

'I know how you must feel but take time to cool down before you go off half-cocked.'

'No one knows how I feel. Have you been beaten up and imprisoned by people that are supposed to be on your side; I don't think so, Sir. May I go and get some sleep and clean up?'

'Yes, we'll talk later.'

After four hours of sleep James woke up and got dressed in his uniform. He felt his face. It still hurt and the eye was partly closed. Women would run a mile from him. Lucky there were no women here!

He went to the mess. He was starving.

'Hello, Cookie, what's on the menu today?'

'Well, you can see it's all there; it's your choice. What happened to you, Sergeant?'

'Bumped into a door; terrible things, doors. I'll have a large cottage pie and veg, please.'

'I'll bring it over to you.'

'Thanks.'

Cookie came over and placed the dinner on the table in front of James.

'That should do the trick. I've put plenty of carrots on there. That's to improve your eyesight so you won't bump into any more doors.'

He went back behind the counter laughing at his own joke. The orderly walked in and came over.

'The Colonel would like to see you in his office, Sergeant. He has Inspector Collins with him.'

'Tell the Colonel with respect I'll see him later but I've nothing to say to the Inspector.'

'He's not going to like it.'

'He don't have to, Corporal.'

'I'll tell him.'

'Thank you.'

James had just finished his dinner when the orderly came back in.

'Sorry, Sergeant, the Colonel said that it wasn't a request but a direct order.'

'We had better go then.'

He put his coffee on the table and walked over to the office with the orderly and knocked on the door. He walked in, stood to attention and saluted.

'Take a seat, Sergeant.'

James sat down, silently looking at the Inspector as he placed a box on the desk.

'These belong to you, Sergeant. I've come to apologize

again and to tell you that when the police sergeant comes out of hospital he will be dealt with. What did you mean when you told him that you have to learn to take it before you dish it out?'

James stood up and opened his combat jacket and showed the scar across his abdomen.

'That's what I mean.'

'How the devil did you get that?'

'Long story, just tell me why you are really here. I think I've done my share to help the RUC, don't you?'

'You mentioned two arms dumps and I would like to know where they're located.'

'But just maybe the Colonel would like to send out two sections and take all the glory for his regiment? What do you say, Colonel?'

The Colonel was rubbing his chin with his hand, deep in thought.

'He's right, you know, Inspector. We could get a lot of good publicity out of this. I can see the headlines now: "Royal Green Jackets find two arms dumps". How long would it take you to get ready, Sergeant?'

'Two hours at the most, including briefing. We could hit while they're having tea and if you are in a generous mood you could ask the RUC to provide backup.'

'You're enjoying this, Sergeant. It's what I would say was rubbing salt into the wound.'

'It was your men who fucked up, I didn't! I had all the information for you. I'm just going for a coffee. It's your call, Colonel.'

As James left he overheard the Colonel speaking to the Inspector.

'Your men picked on the wrong man there to fuck with. He's the hardest bastard I've ever met but since he has been over here the morale in the barracks is sky high. The section I gave him to train is the best I've ever seen and all of them would follow him to hell and back, He's a one-man bleeding army, Inspector …'

James smiled. Nice to be appreciated.

An hour later he was back in the office again. If possible the Inspector looked even more contrite.

'Sit down, Sergeant. I've been giving it a lot of thought. You got the information so you can pick which target you would like to raid and you'll take two RUC officers with you. The other target we'll let the Inspector and his men deal with, all right.'

'If that's what you want to do, Sir, it's fine by me. I'll take the home of Connor Murphy at Head Hill Farm near Keady and the Inspector can take the one near the wood yard.'

'You *were* there then. Why did you kill him the way you did with a circular saw?'

'He cut up a bit rough.'

The Inspector smirked. 'What did I tell you, Colonel, he's getting back to his old self.'

'What do you mean by that, Sir?'

'I told the Colonel that if I asked you why you killed Jerry Wilson you would come back with some witty answer.'

'You're beginning to know me then.' James gave them a description of the whereabouts of the arms dump at the wood yard.

'But how do you know they're not both false trails?'

'I wouldn't stake my life on them being right, but at least two men did.'

'See, you're at it again, Sergeant.'

'Yes, Inspector. Could you hit at 1100 hours tomorrow morning. We'll need to hit them at the same time.'

'That's not a problem; I can arrange that. I'll have your two officers here at 1000 hours. They'll know that they're under your orders. All right, Sergeant?'

James hesitated. 'Colonel, can I ask the Major to come along. It would be fitting if we had a senior officer there. I'm sure that if *you* would like to come along the Inspector would lend you a tank.'

The Inspector was laughing out loud. 'Yes, we've a spare one we could lend you. Welcome back, Sergeant.' He reached across and shook James by the hand.

'You've had your one chance, Inspector. Is that understood?'

'Fine, I understand.'

The Colonel looked at both of them as if they had both gone stark raving bonkers. 'What's this about a bloody tank?'

At 0900 hours the following day the section came in. Corporal Brown had warned them about the operation and they were champing at the bit.

'Good morning, lads. Are you looking forward to this one? This is the first raid that you been on, isn't it?'

'Yes, Sergeant.'

'Right, sit down and then we can get started and as the other people arrive who will be involved we'll bring them up to speed.' James began to give them the details of the plan.

'Corporal Brown, the green pins are where part of your section will end up in. To get to those positions move in, in extended order. I'll take the centre with Major Franklin and the two RUC officers, all right?'

'Yes, Sergeant.'

'Good. Lance Corporal Minter, you are the red pins. You and three men will be dropped off with the GPMG and will move towards the rear of the farmhouse and take up fire positions and cover the rear and both sides of the farm house, all right?'

'Yes, Sergeant.'

Just then the cabin door opened and in walked four soldiers.

'Excuse me, Sergeant, two drivers and two armed escorts were told to report to you.'

'Welcome, boys, are you already paired up?'

'Yes, Sergeant, I'm Private Bush and I'm with Private King. This is Private Lucas and he's with Private Warren.'

'Private Bush and King, you're the black pin and that's where I want the main party dropped off and the lorry to stay there. You'll be issued with a radio and your call sign is Charlie one four, all right.'

'Yes, Sergeant.'

'Privates Lucas and Warren, you're the white pin and that's where I want Lance Corporal Minter dropped off. As soon as you've done that, go to where the black pin is. You won't need a radio because you'll be parked and both lorries will be together, all right?'

'Yes, Sergeant.'

'When you take up your fire positions make sure you know where the rest of the section is. I don't want a blue-on-blue situation, do you all understand?'

'Yes, Sergeant.'

'Once the warrant has been issued and we have control of the situation and we've found the arms, then we'll bring the lorries in and remove the weapons and bring them back here. Now have a look at the map and if you don't understand ask!'

A little later Major Franklin walked over from the office in full kit with two RUC officers in tow.

'Sergeant, this is Constables Nolan and Green. Inspector Collins has sent them over with the search warrant and to do the arresting if there is any to be done.'

'I see you have your own transport, so if you follow the lorry with the main body in it and, when we get out, leave the Land-Rover there. We'll go in on foot with the Major. We'll be in the centre of the line, but keep spread out.'

'The Inspector told us that by the time we got here you would have everything sorted out.'

'I try and that's because I don't like any unpleasant surprises.'

'Tiny, are those radios ready and handed out.'

'Yes, Sergeant.'

'Good one! Let's get this show on the road. Weapons loaded and safety catch on! Believe me, it can save your life. Then when we get back use the unloading bay.'

There was a rattle of weapons being loaded, then they all mounted the vehicles and were on their way.

When they got near Head Hill Farm the two front vehicles turned to go towards the front of the farmhouse, while Lance Corporal Minter's group carried straight on and headed for the rear.

The farmhouse was set back about four hundred metres from the main road. The lorry stopped on the main road – they would advance on foot.

'Tiny, get hold of bravo one four and find out their position. I want everyone to reach their positions at more or less at the same time.'

'Yes, Sergeant.'

There was a track that led from the main road to the farmhouse. James took one side of the track and Constable Green the other; the Major took up his position five metres from James and the other RUC officer five metres away from his colleague. The rest of the section divided in two and took up their positions on either side, keeping the spacing at five metres.

'Sergeant.' It was Tiny. 'Bravo one four are about three hundred metres from the farmhouse at the rear.'

'Fine, tell him to move in and take up fire positions. Corporal Brown, move them forward.'

Keeping their spacing, they moved towards the farm-house. They got to within forty metres when the front door opened and Conor Murphy stood in the doorway with a double-barrel shotgun in his hands.

'What the hell are you doing on my land? Clear off!'

James called out. 'Put the gun on the ground and I'll come forward and talk to you. I know you're a brave man but you're not stupid. You can see you've no chance with the firepower we 'ave.'

Conor Murphy slowly lowered the shotgun to the ground and stood up scowling. James moved forward with the two RUC officers and stood about two metres away. James lowered his weapon so it pointed at the ground as if to pose no threat, Constable Nolan stepped forward.

'Mr Conor Murphy, I've a warrant to search the farmhouse, land and outbuildings known as Head Hill Farm.'

He handed the warrant to Conor, who took it and began to read. He looked as nervous as a kitten.

'Is there anyone else in the house?'

'Only my wife, that's all.'

'Will you ask her to step outside, please?'

'Mavis, can you come outside? They won't hurt you.'

A large woman wearing an apron came outside with her hands covered in flour where she had been baking. She wiped her hands on her apron and stood with her hands on her hips, reminding James of a professional wrestler. She looked at Conor and bellowed.

'What's going on here and what are they here for?'

'These gentlemen have a search warrant to search the farmhouse, land and outbuildings.'

Constable Green stepped forward.

'We'll start with the house first. We'll try not to inconvenience you too much. You can come with us.'

'Too bloody sure!' the woman retorted bitterly. 'I'll want to see that you don't do any damage or plant anything.'

'Why should we plant anything?'

'Because you're Protestants and we're Catholics, that's why.'

'Religion has got nothing to do with it. I'm here to do my job and that's it.'

Still moaning, she went into the house followed by the two RUC officers.

James called to Tiny. 'Get Bravo one four to move and cover the outbuildings. There is no threat here now.'

'Yes, Sergeant.'

Lance Corporal Minter moved his men to cover the milking parlour and the tractor shed and they took up fire positions. The two officers came out of the farmhouse.

'All clear! We can go to the outbuildings now. Mr Murphy, will you please accompany us?'

Without a word Conor walked slowly down to the tractor shed. The tractor shed was quite big and the floor was covered with a scattering of hay. James got the tractors taken outside and four men from the section found forks and started scraping the hay off the floor. They came across an area of timber boards. They prised one board out after another. James moved closer to Conor Murphy; he was getting more and more on edge.

'Look what we have here, Sergeant – it's a little arsenal.'

James pushed Conor to the edge of the pit.

'Let's go and have a look, shall we?'

Constable Nolan took hold of Conor Murphy, read him his rights and handcuffed him. He was led outside. James turned to Tiny.

'Tiny, get on to Charlie one four to bring all the vehicles including the Land-Rover up to the tractor shed.'

'Yes, Sergeant.'

'Let's get this little lot out of the pit. We'll need to make a list of exactly what we have.'

'Sergeant, did you know they have a bloody two-inch mortar here?!'

Major Franklin came over and watched as the pit was emptied and the gear put into piles.

'Well done, Sergeant. That's quite a haul. It will be nice to have them put out of the reach of the IRA.'

'I'm very pleased, Sir. Just imagine the damage those mortars could do if they were lobbed into the barracks, I'm over the moon.'

'Well, you've saved the day again, Sergeant.'

'If we tell you what's there, Sir, can you act as the scribe and make a list?'

'Not your kind of thing, eh, Sergeant, reports and lists?' the Major quipped.

Back at the barracks the Colonel was waiting to greet them. He walked over to Major Franklin.

'Major, did everything go all right?'

'Yes, Sir, we've a load of weapons, explosives and two two-inch mortars and some mortar bombs as well.'

'Brilliant! The more hardware they lose the harder it is for them to go on the offensive.'

'Yes, Sir, but it's a pity they did away with the SLR because we've five thousand rounds of ammo and it would fit them nicely.'

'You're right, Major. They make bigger and better bombs, yet they cut down the calibre of bullets. The SLR was a stopper, even if the shock could kill if you were hit in the arm.'

James joined them. 'Colonel, have you heard how Inspector Collins' raid went?'

'No, I'm still waiting to hear but I'm sure we'll hear soon. As soon as I know, I'll let you know.'

'Thank you, Sir. Major, the lads were wondering as we've had a successful day if you would have dinner with them?'

'Yes, Sergeant, I think that would be a great idea. Let's go, I'm starving.'

They all walked to the mess and the Major went up first and got his dinner and took it over to a table. The rest of the section got their dinners and they all sat together, laughing and joking. The two RUC officers walked in and came over to James.

'Conor Murphy is all locked up safe and sound.'

'Well done! Would you lads like to get yourself a dinner and come and join us?'

'Thank you, Sergeant, that would be more than welcome.'

Just as they were finishing their dinners Colonel Wiseman walked in.

'Relax, gentlemen, I've just come over to thank you all for a job well done and to thank our friends from the RUC as well.'

The boys clapped and cheered.

'Also I've heard from Inspector Collins. His raid was also a great success so we've taken a lot of hardware off the streets of Belfast. If we were allowed alcohol in the base I would buy you all a pint but when we get home if you invite me to your mess you'll get that pint. Thanks again.'

That night in his little room James lay on his bed looking at the piece of paper that Candy had put in his case.

Chapter 12

Two days after the raid the Sergeant was called into the Colonel's office.

'You wanted to see me, Sir?'

'Yes, Sergeant. Take a seat, I've just had Colonel Kelly on the telephone and he said that Corporal Kate Fareway has withdrawn into her shell and refuses to have counselling. He's worried that she might self-harm.' The Colonel hesitated. 'He was wondering if you could do anything to help?'

'I would rather not, Sir, I'm not qualified.'

'We know but you seemed to work wonders with her.'

'Sir, I understand what a state she may be in. I've seen it before. When someone's seen a mate get killed or they've been wounded themselves. All too often, Sir, they're let down by the people that should care, the Army.'

'Yes, I agree with what you are saying, but will you just talk to her?'

'It will take more than a talk, Sir. How long can you spare me for?'

'How long do you reckon it will take, Sergeant?'

'Two or three days, Sir. If I've not achieved anything in that time, then I'm sorry to say that I'll have to give it up as a bad job.'

'Well, I'll talk to Colonel Kelly and tell him that you'll try and that I can spare you for three days.'

'Can I use the unmarked car? I'll have to go to Loughgall where she lives. I'll have to wear civvies and carry no weapons. It will be a risky business just being out and about.'

'I'll arrange it. I don't think it's being used. When could you leave?'

'In about an hour, Sir.'

They agreed that Kate Fareway wouldn't be told about James' role, not at first anyway. He would go over to the Loughgall Barracks and speak to Colonel Kelly first.

At Loughgall James was taken around to the rear of the main building and up a steel fire escape. He was shown into the Colonel's office.

'Hello, Colonel, it's nice to see you again, Sir, but I wish it was under happier circumstances.'

'I wish it was, too, Sergeant, but I would appreciate it if you could find a way to help her.'

'Could you give her three days' leave starting today; only I would like to take her away for a few days. It will give her time to try and pull her socks up and get through the problems and back to her old self.'

'That's fine. As long as it takes, Sergeant. I just hope and pray that she will be all right.'

'I'll do my best, Sir. Have you got a spare office where we can talk alone? If I can persuade her to go away for a bit, I'll come and ask your permission. I don't want her to know we've already spoken.'

'I'll take you to the interview room. You won't be disturbed there.'

As they went out of the office he called over an orderly. 'Corporal, can you go and fetch Corporal Fareway and take her to Interview Room 2 and let her go in on her own?'

'Yes, Sir.'

Colonel Kelly showed James to the interview room two and left him there.

'Good luck, Sergeant. See you later I hope.'

'So do I, Sir.'

James sat in the chair behind a desk, then changed his

mind. The desk would be a barrier and he wanted to put her at ease. The door opened and she walked in eyes looking at the floor.

'Don't you want to look at me, Corporal Kate Fareway?'

'James, what are you doing here?'

'I came to see you. Don't I get a hug then?'

She moved quickly and threw her arms around him, and he held her tight and close to him.

'How have you been? Are you keeping well?'

'Not really. I'm trying to get back to normal but it's not as easy as I thought it would be. What are you really doing here, James?'

'Well, that depends on you.'

'What do you mean, it depends on me?'

'Well, I've three days off and I wondered if I can get you three days off. We could get away and spend some time together. What do you think of that?'

'The Colonel would never let me have the time off. He's a stickler for the rules; it would never work.'

'If I can swing it with the Colonel, would you like to go and have some fun. No guns, I promise!'

'I would love to go but it's not going to happen.'

'You are just being a pessimist. The Colonel owes me one for saving your bacon, so look on the bright side. Shall we give it a go? Come on, let's go and see him.'

'All right then.'

He took hold of her hand and they went to the Colonel's office and knocked on the door. James looked at Kate and smiled.

'Come in.'

They walked in. The Colonel feigned surprise. 'Well, hello, Sergeant! And how are you?'

'Never been better, Sir. Why I've come to see you is I've got three days off. Not long enough to go home but I was wondering if Corporal Fareway could have three days

off, then we could catch up on old times and have some
fun?'

'Yes, I think we can manage without her for a few days. I
don't think the whole of the Ulster Defence Regiment will
come to a grinding halt. Enjoy yourselves.'

Kate could hardly contain her astonishment.

'That's very good of you and thanks, Sir,' James said.

Corporal Fareway stood to attention and saluted. As they
went out of the door he turned to the Colonel and winked.
So far so good.

Outside the office he turned to Kate.

'I told you to look on the bright side. Let's go and get your
clothes packed and get on our way.'

Kate was dumbstruck.

Kate's parents' house was just a couple of miles away. James
waited outside while Kate went indoors to change her clothes
and pack her case. 'Will you not come in and meet my
parents?' she had asked.

'No, it's better if I stay with the car. Tell them you're going
away on a training course.'

Kate got out of the car and twenty minutes later she came
back. She was wearing a white silk blouse that made her red
hair shine. She had a light-grey skirt that finished about two
inches above the knee and black semi-high-heeled shoes. She
looked stunning but her eyes spoiled things – they had lost
all their sparkle.

They crossed the border into the Republic and headed for
Dundalk, then Drogheda. Kate had fallen asleep and her
breasts were rising and falling with the rhythm of her
breathing.

Just before Drogheda, James turned off and headed for
Clogger. There he spotted a small estate agent's. It was like
someone's front room but had a large window with pictures
of houses for sale. James left Kate sleeping in the car and
walked in. A smart-looking lady was sitting behind a desk.

'Hello, Sir. Can I help you?'

'I hope so. Have you got a cottage or holiday flat to rent for three days on your books, please?'

'Wait a minute … It might be your lucky day, I think. I've a cottage that was booked and they didn't turn up. Let me have a look.' She got up, showing quite a bit of leg, not that James was complaining. She went to a filing cabinet and pulled out a file and placed it on the desk.

'Yes, here it is. It's small and only has one bedroom, but I can let you have it for three days for the price of two. It would be one hundred and twenty pounds plus sixty pounds deposit, which you'll get back once you hand back the key. Is that all right?'

As she busied herself with the paperwork, she spotted his admiring glances. She showed even more leg and smiled.

'Do you like what you see?'

'Best pair of pins I've seen in a long time. Have you got any jobs going, like sharpening pencils?'

'Not really.'

'That's a shame; I could look at them all day.'

'You're such a charmer. I'll get the key for you.'

She got up and went into the other room and came back with the key and gave it to James.

'Thank you. Can you tell me how to get there?'

She gave him the instructions then sat down at the desk again. She gave James a strange look.

'Well, that's it, we've finished. Can I ask what you are waiting for?'

'I was just waiting for you to put the file back in the filing cabinet and then I'll go.'

'All right then.'

She got up and pulled her skirt up as high as she dared and went and put the file back.

'And when you bring the key back I might even show you more than you bargained for.'

'Promises! See you later.'

James drove towards Clogger and just past the pub turned left and parked outside number 22. He shook Kate awake and she smiled when she saw the quaint-looking cottage where the last of the summer's flowers still lingered in the tiny front garden.

While Kate was unpacking her case, James went to the fish shop and got two cod and chips and on the way back he called into a little corner shop and bought some provisions. When he got back Kate was curled up on the settee in the twilight. She seemed to be retreating back into her shell and she wasn't talking. James put his arm around her. She looked up and gave him a half-hearted smile.

'What's troubling you? You've gone into your shell. Will you talk to me about it?'

'No I can't, James; it's too frightening! I have such horrible dreams in which I think I'm going to die and I'm really scared.'

'Come on, tell me everything. You'll find I'm a very good listener and while you're telling me I'll hold you. You're safe. We have to talk it through if you're going to move on.'

'No, no! I'm going to bed.'

'All right, go to bed but it won't help you slay those dragons that are running around in your mind.'

James stood at the bottom of the stairs and could hear her sobbing. After about ten minutes she had fallen asleep. He settled down on the sofa and pulled a blanket over himself.

He must have fallen asleep, because it seemed only a moment later that he was woken by screaming. He ran up the stairs two at a time and rushed over to the bed. She was running with sweat.

'What's the matter? I'm not leaving here until you tell me, so what's it going to be?'

Her fingers dug into his arms and she laid her head on his chest. She was holding on tight.

'I think I'm going mad. My mind is playing tricks and I've a job to know what's true and what's a lie. Do you know what I mean?'

'Not really but if you start at the beginning and just maybe we'll work out what's going on in that head of yours.'

'You know when you saved me and we lay together in your room; well, I lay beside you hoping that you would touch me even though … even though I was a virgin. I just wanted to grab you and feel you inside and that was wrong. You had killed for me and all I wanted to do was jump on your bones. It's because I had such dirty thoughts that I'm being punished! I have the same nightmare every night. I'm lying in a coffin and the lid is screwed down and it's all black and I'm lying in the darkness. I can feel the heat of the fire but before the coffin gets burnt I have an out-of-body experience. I see my headstone and the inscription reads: "In loving memory. Here lies Kate Fareway." The dates are never clear! Then I wake up sweating and screaming. Oh James. I know I'm going to die. I'm being punished!'

'Now let's put all this in perspective, one piece at a time. When I came to rescue you, despite all the horror, I fancied you like crazy. I couldn't help myself. I could have taken you then and there. You know, however terrible a situation is you can't help having feelings, however inappropriate they may seem. We just have to put them aside and get on with things. You're being too hard on yourself, Kate.'

'But I've never felt like that before.'

'You're a woman, Kate, and you want to be loved, cuddled and made love to … told that everything is going to be all right … That's feelings.'

'But what can I do about feelings like that, they're twisting my mind!'

'You'll know when the time is right, and this dream you're having, well, you don't want to go to your grave without experiencing life and love and the feeling of being wanted.

The dates you can't see because they're so far ahead in the future they're just a mist and at this moment count for nothing.

'Now have a shower and think about what I've said and I'll bring you a cup of coffee. White one sugar, am I right?'

'Yes, spot on. Thank you!'

James went downstairs and into the kitchen and made the coffee. He heard her footsteps go back into the bedroom and he called up the stairs.

'Are you ready for your coffee?'

'Yes please.'

He took it upstairs and handed it to her and she put it on the bedside cabinet. He sat on the edge of the bed.

'Do you feel any better?'

'Yes but will you lay beside me just in case those gremlins decide to come back again?'

'Yes of course I will.'

James stripped off down to his boxer shorts and got into bed. He felt her skin against his. She was naked. She held his hand and laid it on her breast. He stroked her nipples and they responded to the touch and came out to play. She kissed him and pulled him close.

'Will you take me, please. I want to feel you inside me. I want to be a real woman and have feelings that are real.'

'You are all woman, a beautiful woman, but before we do you must know it can't go anywhere.'

'I understand but I still want you more than ever.'

He placed his hand between her legs and touched her. She was wet and receptive. He lay on top and pushed gently. She gave out a cry and started moving her body up and down. He kissed her neck and she started moving faster and faster. Then all of a sudden she arched her back and gave out a shout of delight – she had reached a climax. James went to get off.

'Lie still for a while,' she pleaded. 'Let me feel you in me for a bit longer; that was fantastic. I didn't think it would ever be like that. It seemed as if you were part of me, thank you.'

James held her close to him. She lay with her head on his chest and was soon fast asleep.

The following morning they decided to go down to the beach. The air was fresh and clean, and despite it being late summer the sun still gave a pleasant warmth. As they walked down the road towards the beach Kate chatted about her life.

'I've always been shy, I get very nervous just talking to men and my parents always want to vet anyone that I choose and it gets very embarrassing.'

'You'll have to stand up to your parents. I know it's not easy but they can't live your life for you. So what have you been doing all this time instead of going out?'

'Most nights when I'm not on duty I just watch films. I have to watch them in my bedroom, so they can watch the television.'

'Now if you could do anything you wanted to do tonight what would it be?'

'I think it would have to be dancing; that would be my number one choice.'

They went over the seawall. Kate kicked her shoes off and ran along the beach. James picked the shoes up and sat on the beach looking at her. It was like watching a child at the seaside for the very first time – she seemed so happy and carefree. He took off his own shoes and socks and walked to the water's edge. He stepped in and the water lapped around his ankles. The water was quite warm. Kate came running over and stood beside him.

'It's lovely here. I'm really enjoying myself and I don't want it to ever end.'

'All things come to an end but other things take their place. You wait and see.'

'I hope so.'

She was kicking the water and jumping up and down.

'Did you bring a dress with you?'

'Why do you want to know?'

'Come on, just tell me.'

'Yes, a black one with a halter neck. You know they tie or are pinned at the back of the neck.'

'You had me worried. I thought horses wore them.'

'You bugger! Are you calling me a horse?'

She kicked water over him. James picked her up and made as if to throw her in the sea. She screamed and clung on to his neck.

James put her down. 'Will you be all right while I make a phone call? I noticed a phone box just over the seawall as we were coming down?'

'Yes I'll stay here and carry on paddling. Is that all right?'

'Of course. I'll not be long.'

He walked to the phone box.

'Hello, Clogger Estate Agents. How can I help you?'

'Is that the lady with the lovely legs?'

'Mr MacDonald! Is there anything wrong with the house?'

'Oh no, I just wanted to know if there is a ladies' hair-dresser's near here that could fit someone in today for the full works. You know what I mean?'

'Yes I do. There's the one I use. It's about four hundred metres from the shop. Is it for your girlfriend?'

'She's not my girlfriend. Just someone who's had it pretty rough lately and I'm trying to snap her back to how she used to be – happy-go-lucky.'

'What is your number there? I'll ring them up now and then ring you back in a minute if they have a booking.'

'Yes, please, the number's Clogger 397. I was also wondering whether there's any pubs around here that have live bands that are playing tonight and a dance floor? Tall order, I know.'

'Leave it with me and I'll get back to you as soon as possible.'

Within a couple of minutes the phone rang.

'Mr MacDonald?'

'James, please.'

'Well, James, I've booked her in for two this afternoon. The pub might take a little longer but when I know I'll put it in an envelope and give it to your friend when she's at the hairdresser's.'

'That's fine, thank you very much. Maybe I'll be able to help you one day.'

'You never know. Bye.'

James replaced the receiver and went back to find Kate. She was still in the water.

'Sorry I was so long. Only all the lines were busy and it took a while to get though. But I'm back now.'

'That's all right. I've been enjoying myself and thinking about when I was a little and we went on holiday. I forgot the name of the place but it was a lot like this.'

'We'll go and get some food because later I've a surprise for you and I think you'll like it.'

'What is it?'

'You'll have to wait and see. I'll keep you on tenterhooks for a while longer.'

'You're a pig.'

'No, I'm not. Anyhow it's better than being a horse and having to wear a halter but I bet the blinkers would suit you.'

She gave him a punch.

'You always have an answer for everything and you're not a very nice man at all.'

On the way back through the village, James suddenly stopped outside the hairdresser's. He looked at her and smiled.

'Well, come on then, we're going to let them change you into a beautiful young lady. What do you think of that?'

'But I don't have an appointment ...' she began.

'Yes you do!'

While Kate got the works, James returned to the cottage and made a cup of black coffee and went to sit on the settee. He heard a car pull up outside. He looked out of the window. The driver's door opened and the first thing he saw was a shapely leg. The crafty bitch! No wonder she wanted to make the appointment for Kate.

He opened the front door and made out that he was surprised to see her. She smiled.

'I thought I'd bring the envelope here instead. I've written down the name of the pub and the name of the band that's playing there tonight.'

James grinned. 'Can I get you a drink?'

'I'll have a glass of water, if I may.'

James went and got a glass of water and placed it on the coffee table. She handed him the piece of paper and it fell on the floor. She bent down to pick it up and her skirt lifted high enough to show the bottom of her knickers and her rounded cheeks. She handed him the paper and then picked up the glass of water but as she went to sit down she threw it all over herself. She jumped up quickly.

'I'm sorry! What a silly thing to do.'

'Hang on and I'll get you a towel.'

He went to his case and pulled out a bath towel and gave it to her. She started dabbing away at her clothes.

'I'm soaked right through to the skin. What am I going to do?'

'Well, if you take them off I'll put them in front of the oven on a couple of stools.'

'That's a good idea. They should dry fairly quickly but not too close, mind. I don't want them to burn.'

By the time James came back into the living room, she had taken off her blouse and skirt as well and he went back into the kitchen and put them with the other clothes. When he returned she was drying her legs and the exposed parts of her body. James approached her and touched her knickers and bra.

'They're wet as well. Hold the bath towel around you and I'll take them off for you.'

She held the bath towel around herself and he undid the back of the bra and she slid it off her arms. He reached up under the bath towel and pulled her knickers down and she stepped out of them. He took them out to the kitchen, while she sat down on the settee with the towel wrapped around her.

'James, I'm sorry. I was so nervous and spilt the water. I did come around to flirt and to see what would happen, but I've spoilt everything. You must think I'm stupid?'

'Why have you spoilt everything. It was the perfect subterfuge! Look at you! I don't even know your name.'

'It's Gwen Walsh.'

'Well, Gwen, have you ever been married and have you got any children?'

'I've been married twice but I got shot of them. They were cheating on me and that was it. I never cheated on either of them. Have you ever been married?'

'Yes, quite a while ago. It didn't work out. I was away too much so she left. She's married with a couple of boys and she seems very happy with her life.'

'I would have loved to have had kids!'

They were silent for a moment.

'Well, Gwen, now you are here what would you like to do? We could play strip poker but I think that I would have an unfair advantage.'

Gwen laughed, embarrassed.

'Look, I've not had sex for a long time and I would love to have sex with you but I don't want you to think that I'm a tart.'

'Now why should I think that? I just think that you could have any man that you wanted. You've a lot to offer.'

'Then I want you.'

James knelt on the floor in front of her and pulled at the knot of the bath towel. Her breasts were firm and well rounded and the nipples were large though they needed some work done on them. He pushed her legs apart and moved forward. He bent over and slowly sucked on the nipples; she was moaning with pleasure. He pulled off his shirt and dropped his jeans and his boxers, then knelt back down again. He put his hands under her buttocks and slid her forward on the settee. Once he was in the right position he pushed forward and entered her. She gave out a grunt and put her legs around his waist but not tight enough to stop him from moving. Her eyes had been closed but now they were open and James was moving in and out faster and faster.

'Come on, big boy ... give it to me ... give it to me!'

Then she cried out and her body went rigid and her legs squeezed him so tight that it felt as if his ribs would break. She had trapped him inside her! Finally she released him and he pulled out and wiped himself on the bath towel and pulled his boxers and jeans up. She had her eyes closed again. She was still in the same position with her legs apart so he touched her and it was still alive.

'No more, James, I can't take any more!'

She sat up and wiped herself gingerly below as well as between her breasts where the sweat ran down her cleavage. James looked at his watch. There was another hour to go before he had to pick Kate up.

'Would you like another drink? But don't throw it all over yourself this time!'

James busied himself in the kitchen, Gwen got herself dressed.

'What will your boss say being away from the office for so long. Will he tell you off?'

'No. He's a she and I'm the boss. I'll have to tell myself off.'

159

'How long have you been in business?'

'I set it up five years ago when I got rid of my second husband.'

She made the final adjustments to her clothes, smoothing out her skirt and arranging her hair.

'Well done! I admire a woman who can make her own way in life and has her own independence.'

'I'd better go now, but I wish I was going to the ball with you! Your friend's lucky to have someone like you to care for her!'

That evening James nearly missed the entrance to The Four Leaf Clover because he was looking for a normal pub; this was more like a castle! Gwen certainly had good taste.

He pulled into the drive and parked near the main steps. He got out and went around and held the door open. Kate got out and he held out his arm and escorted her in through to the bar. She looked gorgeous, like a princess. Her red hair was shoulder-length and shiny, with a fringe that came just above her eyes. He noticed with pleasure that they were sparkling again.

'What would you like to drink?'

'Just an orange juice, please.'

James went to the bar and ordered an orange juice and a half of lager. As he paid for the drinks he asked, 'Do you have a restaurant?'

'Yes, Sir, through those big doors at the far end, next to the Ballroom. There's a sign over the doors.'

'Many thanks.'

They took the drinks and sat at a table with plush leather chairs around it.

'I've never been to anywhere as posh as this. The dances I go to are just at country pubs with a small dance floor. I feel a little bit out of place and people are looking at me.'

'You're not out of place. People are looking because

you're the most beautiful thing in the room. Relax, It's your evening, Kate.'

At dinner James ordered a bottle of sparkling white wine.

'Are you trying to get me drunk, so you can have your wicked way with me?'

'Do I have to get you drunk for that then?'

She smiled but didn't answer. They were sipping the cool, white wine when a waiter waved and beckoned him over. James got up and walked over to him.

'You want me?'

'Yes, are you Mr MacDonald?'

'Yes, why do you want to know?'

'Your meals have already been paid for and the lady said enjoy the dance but save the last dance for her.'

James went back to the table and sat down.

'What did he want you for?'

'He just said that you lighted up the whole room and it was a pleasure to serve you.'

'That was nice of him.'

'Shall we dance the night away?'

'Yes, come on then.'

Kate stood up and grabbed his hand and they went through to the ballroom and on to the dance floor. He put his arm around her and they danced around the floor. He could tell by her eyes that she was happy and enjoying herself. After about half a dozen dances they went and sat down for a rest, then a young man came over and asked her for a dance. She looked at James.

'Go on! If you want to dance, dance! I told you tonight is your night. Enjoy yourself!'

During the evening Kate ended up dancing with quite a few young men. It was ten to midnight when Kate came over, still breathless from her last dance.

'Is it time to go back yet?'

'Yes but not before I have the last dance with you. Don't

you remember the song: "You can dance with the guy, who gives you the eye, but don't forget who's taking you home, so darling save the last dance for me."'

Kate smiled. 'Come on then this one's for you, then we'll have to go. But I have to say, James, it's been the best day of my life. I feel like I'm starting all over again.'

They walked over to the dance floor and he held her close. She put her head against his face and together they swayed to the music.

Chapter 13

It was 1930 hours and almost dark when James reached Dermot McNally's – Four Oaks Farm near Portadown. The fields around the house were large and, although they had hedges around them, they didn't go close enough to the farmhouse for him to be able to get a good view. His only hope of getting a good view was to use one of the oak trees as a vantage point. It wasn't ideal, but needs must.

The house was quite a modern one and quite large. A perimeter fence ran all the way around the house, at about twenty-five metres. It was three metres high and it was a chain-link fence. A farm track ran past the front of the house inside the fence and there were double gates. There was six halogen security lights fitted to poles close to the fence, four shining into the compound and two shining up and down the track. Just outside the perimeter fence was a big old shed – a milking parlour, James presumed from the large grey-metal tanks that stood nearby.

There was no movement from the farmhouse, although there were lights in some of the downstairs windows. After about an hour and being stuck up a tree, James found his bottom going numb and his legs were beginning to ache; he slowly shifted position to try to ease the discomfort. He kept looking through his binoculars. Still nothing,

He heard it before he could see it. There was a cattle lorry coming up the track. Two men came out of the house and opened the double gates and the cattle lorry entered the compound and stopped. There were two men in the lorry but James was unable to see their faces because of the glare from the security lights.

A man jumped out of the passenger side, and James nearly fell out of the tree.

Tim 'The Tank' Sherman.

The man who had trained James and taught him all he knew. Bloody Sherman was the mole! He couldn't believe his eyes. Sherman!

But why? Why had he turned traitor? Sherman had been like a father to him.

The driver got out and lowered the tailgate and walked up the ramp and drove about half a dozen cows out of the back. The tailgate was shut and the lorry reversed up to two haystacks. Some of the bales were removed from the side of a haystack and a door was opened. A concealed outbuilding. It must have been a shed with bales of hay piled up around it, the crafty bastards! The lorry was unloaded and what looked distinctly like arms and ammo was put inside.

James had seen enough. Now came the difficult bit. He would have to get down from the tree without being seen. He almost fell rather than climbed down from his perch and he stood behind the tree and rubbed his bottom and legs until the pins and needles were gone. He made his way back to his car and thought for a moment. He wanted to tail the lorry to see where it went to or really to see where The Tank was going.

James drove to a crossroads and parked up so he could see the main road. He cut the lights and engine and sat back to wait, his mind wandering back to his time with The Tank. He remembered a really cold night in December and the wind was blowing and the snow was driving straight into his face. The snow on his combats was being melted by his body heat and in no time you were soaked right through. They had only done twenty miles and there was still another fifteen to do to get to the finishing line. James had turned to The Tank and said, 'I can't make it. I've taken all I can.'

'If you stop, boy, you'll die out here and there will be no gravestone because I'll not be coming back for you! So pick yourself up! One foot in front of the other, every one you take will take you nearer to the finishing line.'

'I don't think I can.'

'You fucking will, boy. Now be a man and not a wimp.'

'You bastard, you fucking bastard!'

'There's still fight in you. Let's sing, how about five thousand green bottles hanging on a wall; that should just about get us there.'

At last they were over the finishing line. Sherman grinned. 'I told you you could do it. At 0600 I want you over the gym for endurance training.'

At 0600 James, who was only a trooper then, was tipped out of bed. The Tank was standing over him.

'Come on, get up out the sack, T-shirt and shorts and over the gym in five!'

James got up off the floor moaning and groaning and ran to the gym. To keep The Tank waiting was unheard of.

'Come on, you wimp, we'll get you fit so you can finish what you start.'

They were doing warm-up exercises and stretching. When they had finished The Tank ordered him to lie on his back on the floor.

He picked up a medicine ball and slammed it into his solar plexus so hard that it knocked all the wind out of him; it made him feel sick.

'Now throw it back, come on.'

James grimaced with pain and threw it back. The exercise was repeated about half a dozen times. Although it hurt like hell, James refused to give in.

This had been repeated every morning for a month and in the end it didn't even hurt and the muscles in his stomach looked like a knotted rope. When James looked back he realized that he had never ever said 'I give up' again, except when he'd been shot in the leg. He had been with The Tank right up until four years ago and then he was transferred to Captain Stony Burkes' team with Willie and Ginger.

The Tank also taught him camouflage, how to be a bloody chameleon and blend in with the surrounding area, how to use the shadows. James could move at night without being seen and the Tank said if you did see him you were dead anyway.

The memories kept flooding back, like the time in the Northern Ireland House, at Hythe used for hostage situations and once you were good enough with a nine millimetre pistol, they would give live ammo and one of your own men would be amongst the targets hoping that you didn't shoot him, in the end James could fire two shots standing, two kneeling and two lying all hitting the target within five seconds.

James looked at his watch. It was 2345 hours. Maybe he had guessed wrong and the lorry had headed for Newry and not Portadown. He would give it another thirty minutes then go.

He was just thinking of calling it a night, when he saw the headlights of the lorry. He waited until it had passed the crossroads. James started the car and pulled out behind the lorry, keeping back and with no lights showing. He was driving by the light of the moon. It was dodgy but at least the lorry was keeping well within the speed limit.

As they approached Portadown, James stopped just past a turning on the left, reversed back into it, put his lights on and pulled back out of the turning. This was to fool them in the lorry; if they were looking in their mirrors they would think he was just a local who had just pulled out on to the main road. On the main street in Portadown the lorry stopped but James kept going. In his mirrors he watched The Tank get out of the lorry and go inside a building. He turned into the next left and switched off the engine and lights. He watched as the lorry passed the side road. Where it was going now he didn't really care – he had found his mole. He waited for about thirty minutes and then drove slowly back past the doorway which the Tank had entered. It was a flat over a mobile phone shop. His brain was working overtime – the shop could easily be cover for a bomb-making factory.

Well, that was enough for tonight.

James was awake and up at 0800. He washed and shaved, put on his uniform and went to the mess for breakfast.

'Hello, Cookie.'

'Hello, Sergeant. Full English, yes?'

'Yes, please.'

'I'll get it for you.'

'Thanks, Cookie.'

'I can see those carrots have worked. You've not bumped into any doors lately.'

'How do you know it was the bloody carrots that worked? It's just an old wives' tale.'

'No it's not! Have you ever seen a rabbit wearing glasses?'

'No, you're right.'

James smiled and Cookie went away laughing. After breakfast James walked over to the office and saw the orderly.

'Hello, Corporal, is the Colonel in?'

'Yes, Sergeant, I'll ring through.'

James went in.

'Good morning, Sir, may I use the red phone? I have to ring Major Tompsett.'

'Yes, Sergeant, you go ahead.'

James rang through to Hereford and waited a couple of minutes.

'Hello, Major Tompsett speaking.'

'Hello, Major, it's Sergeant MacDonald. I've some news for you and you're not going to like it. The mole is an ex-SAS captain, Tim Sherman. I heard he was busted to sergeant about two years ago and left after a bust-up with a senior officer.'

'Are you sure about this, Sergeant?'

'Yes, Sir, I've seen him with my own eyes.' James explained what he had seen the night before.

'Bloody hell! I'll have to report this to Colonel Hickly to see what he wants to do. Will you be in the office? I'll get back to you as soon as I can.'

'Yes, Sir, I'll wait for you to get back to me.'

James put the receiver down and phoned through to Loughgall and Major Randall.

Once again he explained the situation. There was the same incredulity followed by horror. One of their own – a mole!

'Can you please find out all you can about a mobile phone shop in the main street in Portadown? Only I think it has connections with the IRA.'

'I'll see what I can find out. I still can't believe it. Sherman was one of the best!'

James put the receiver back deep in thought. Colonel Wiseman had listened to James' tail with evident interest.

'Quite a man this Tank Sherman, obviously. What made him go over to the other side do you know?'

'Well, I've got a good idea but I intend to find out. He was like a father to me, Sir. He taught me everything I know. He was fearless and led from the front. He was the real thing, Sir.'

The phone rang and the Colonel answered it and passed it to James. 'For you, Sergeant.'

'I've spoken to Colonel Hickly. He said that the name of the regiment is at stake and if he's arrested it will be in every newspaper here and in Northern Ireland. The Colonel wants him taken out without any fuss. Correction: he wants *you* to take him out.'

James felt a wave of anger. 'Why me? He knows how good

The Tank is and that's why he passes me the shit end of the stick. Another way to try to get rid of me.'

'Don't tell me you're frightened of Sherman. You know the Colonel will only order you to do it.'

'I fear no one, Sir. I can look after myself, but I'd prefer the order in writing, Major, because if anything goes wrong he'll throw me to the wolves and have no qualms about it.'

'You know he will never put it in writing. He may be a fool but not that big a fool.'

'Then tell the Colonel that if I go head to head against the Tank then I want something in return and that's that Captain Burke is put down as having been killed in action and Jill gets a widow's pension. That's my offer, take it or leave it! Get back to me as soon as possible, Sir, and let me know if he accepts.'

James almost slammed down the phone. He had steam coming out of his ears.

'Sergeant, take it easy and remember he's your Commanding Officer. I wouldn't stand for you talking about me like that!'

'I don't think I would ever have to, Sir, because, as I've told you, you're a gentleman and I think your word is your bond. May I ask you a question, Sir?'

'Yes, go on.'

'Would you ask one of your soldiers to commit murder just to save the name of your regiment?'

'No, I don't think I would. I think I would play it by the book.'

'You knew Captain Burke well. Do you know how he died?'

'I was told by Major Tompsett that he died in a road traffic accident near his home.'

'One of my first jobs when I came back was to go to Captain Burke's and his daughter Nikki's funeral and to go to the police and then report my findings. Well, he was crashed into by a stolen lorry and it was a deliberate act and I found out how it was done and put in a report to that effect, but I was told by the CO that it would be filed as a tragic accident. I think that, when he was over here, he must have been getting too close to the truth so the IRA had him assassinated. At the very least his wife should be getting a pension but they keep on about it being a tragic accident! What the bloody hell is the Army coming to?'

'One bad apple can make the rest of the barrel go rotten but one man does not make a regiment.'

The red phone started to ring and he passed it to James. 'Colonel Hickly for you.'

James put his hand over the mouthpiece.

'Can you listen in on this, please?'

James twisted the phone around so that the Colonel could hear the conversation.

'Hello, Colonel.'

'Hello, Sergeant, who the devil do you think you are and what are you trying to achieve with all these conditions?'

'Justice, Sir, you want me to kill The Tank, don't you? Well I want justice for Jill Burke. She deserves that and so does Captain Burke.'

'And if I say I'll do my best to get Jill a pension you'll go against Sherman?'

'Let me ask you a question, Sir: would *you* ever go against Tim Sherman on equal terms?'

'You know I wouldn't, You're the trained soldier and that's your job. You're enjoying this, Sergeant.'

'The fuck I am, Sir. Do I have your word that whatever happens you'll do everything to get Jill her pension?'

'Yes, you have my word.'

'All right I'll do my best but it's not for you; it's for Captain Burke and his wife.'

James put the phone back and turned to face the Colonel.

'He's a joke! I don't know what you think but this is the man meant to be in charge of an elite regiment.'

'I must say that I'm not impressed, but I'm with you here. You can count on me as a lever if anything does go wrong.'

A short while later Major Randall rang. The mobile phone shop and building, it seemed, were owned by a Michael Finn. Oddly the shop wasn't making much money at all but just breaking even. Finn had no known connections to any IRA members but that didn't prove much. It could easily be a cover operation. The Major also had some more interesting news.

'I also have the Army records on Sergeant Tim Sherman and a transcript of the trial. You're not going to like it. At the trial it was claimed that during an operation Sherman shot and killed an Irishman. He said he had no choice because he had pulled a gun but the only thing is no gun was found at the scene. Your friend Colonel Hickly, who was a Major then and in charge of the court, gave Sergeant Sherman a choice: if he resigned without a fuss then it would be swept under the carpet; if not, it would go to court and he would be charged with murder. So Sherman resigned and left the Army. The only way I could get a transcript was by threatening that new evidence had come to light.'

'Well done, Major. Colonel Hickly has a lot to answer but that still doesn't excuse going over to the other side and getting your own mates killed. It's just like squeezing the trigger yourself.'

'If any more information comes through I'll be in touch. Good luck! You are going to need all you can get.'

'Thank you, Major, I'll be in touch. Goodbye.'

At 0900 James picked up the unmarked car from the MT shed and headed for Portadown. He found a car park just off the high street and walked to the mobile phone shop. Inside a young woman was sitting behind the counter reading a book. There were no customers and no one else in the shop.

James walked past. On the opposite of the road was a café

171

with two aluminium tables outside. A woman in her early forties, with black hair and a well-rounded figure, was busy wiping the tables. It was a dingy-looking place but obviously very clean.

James walked past and went into a newsagent's and bought a southern Irish newspaper. He put it under his arm and slowly walked back down the street until he got to the café, He opened the door and walked in.

'Good morning, Sir, what would you like?'

James looked at the notice board. There was an all-day breakfast and a special – liver, bacon, onions, mash and gravy.

'Black coffee, please, and I'll have the special.'

'If you would like to take a seat I'll bring it over to you.'

'Thank you very much.'

James paid for the meal and picked a table. He sat with his back to the wall and where he could see the mobile phone shop. The woman brought the meal over and placed it on the table in front of him.

'Thank you. That looks great.'

It tasted fantastic – he had forgotten what this old classic tasted like.

James was still watching the mobile phone shop when the door opened and Tim Sherman came out onto the main street and walked towards the café, James lifted the paper up and pretended to be reading it. Was luck with him? Was Tim coming into the café? If so, he could confront him in the café rather than having to follow him and try to pick a place somewhere else. This was ideal.

The door opened and Tim walked in and went to the counter and ordered a full breakfast. The woman disappeared into the kitchen.

'Hello, Tim, don't do anything silly or I'll blow your balls off – and you know that I can. I just want to talk.'

'I knew they would send someone but I never guessed it would be you! Sending a boy to do a man's job.'

'It's no good, Tim. You're only trying to goad me. Remember, you were the one who taught me and you did a damn good job of it.'

'You learned fast though it doesn't mean you're better than the master.'

'Why did you cross the line and go over to the other side? I always thought you were a man of principles and loyalty, especially towards your mates. Tell me why?'

The woman came over and placed the breakfast in front of Tim and James moved over to his table.

'I'll have a coffee, please, and stick it on his tab,' James said.

'You two know each other?'

'Yes, from way back. Stick it on my bill, love, that's the least I can do for him,' Tim said, with a slight jeer.

She poured a cup of coffee and brought it over to the table.

'Thank you.'

She then went back into the kitchen and Tim started eating his breakfast.

'Now tell me why?'

'You know why! I swear to you, James, there was a gun and that's why I fired. But no gun was found; the only thing I can think might have happened is that in the confusion one of his mates took the gun and ran off.'

'I believe you, Tim, but why didn't you fight it through the courts and let them decide.'

'Who do you think they would believe – a captain that had been busted to sergeant or a major who had an unblemished record?'

'I still can't condone what your lot did to Stony. He was a friend of yours as well as mine.'

'Stony was getting too close and it was either him or me. They said they would make it look like an accident.'

'They fucked up. The accident site had IRA stamped all

over it, and did they tell you that they killed his daughter as well? She hadn't done anything wrong.'

James looked straight into Tim's eyes. He could tell that he hadn't been told. He even thought he could see a tear.

'No, I was just told that it was done and there would be no more problems and we would carry on.'

'Now why become a turncoat and give the IRA information that lost us a lot of men?'

'I tried to get a job when I left and all I could get was work as a security guard looking after an aircraft factory. I needed the money and I would have gone mad if I had worked there any longer.'

'Don't you feel any remorse, Tim? I used to look up to you. You were like the father I never had. But not anymore. I look upon you as the lowest of the low, the stuff you wipe off the bottom of your shoe.'

'I'm sorry it's come to this, James, but you hold all the aces so what happens next? I know you're not going to kill me now, so what have you got planned?'

'Tell me who you work for. I'll find out one way or another and then I'll tell you.'

'You know I can't tell you that.'

'Well, I'll play you for it then. You know that I've no choice but to come after you, so I'm going to give you a fighting chance. We'll both start on a level playing field. You know the wood yard at Market Hill, opposite The Ulsterman's Arms?'

'Yes, I've been there.'

'Well, the back of the wood yard is the start of the killing ground. A quarter of a mile into the wood and a quarter of a mile from the right-hand side of the wood yard, that's the zone we'll fight in. Are you with me so far?'

'Yes, go on.'

'I'll be there from 2000 until 2200 so we have two hours to find each other and get the job done. On the way in I want you to put the name of the man you're working for in an envelope and wedge it into the gate of the wood yard. If you win you can pick it up again on your way out and if I win I'll do the same. Do you agree and do I have your word – no tricks?'

'Two more coffees, please, love,' Tim shouted over.

The woman made the coffees and brought them over to the table. Tim looked at James.

'Can I trust you, James. You hold all the cards at the moment?'

'Just remember that I could have killed you as soon as you walked though that door. This way you've a chance and if you don't show you know that I'll track you down and you'll have no chance at all. This is your one chance to walk away. What do you say?'

'All right, James, but just pray because tomorrow night will be your last on this earth. But you have my word – no tricks; it will be a fair fight, the fight of the century.'

James stood up and turned to the woman behind the counter.

'Thanks for the meal. It was just like my mother use to make. Better!'

'You should try my Irish stew with dumplings,' she said with a smile.

'I can imagine that and the dumplings don't look too bad from over here.'

'You cheeky thing!'

He turned back to Tim.

'Tomorrow night, yes?'

'Yes, I'll be there.'

Chapter 14

Back at the barracks, James went straight to the Colour Sergeant.

'Have you got a camouflage cape and a night sight for the SA80?'

'Yes, I think I can do that, Sergeant. Are you going on one of your night-time expeditions that we keep hearing about.'

'Yes, want to come with me?'

'Not bloody likely.'

The Colour Sergeant found what he wanted. 'Sign here.'

James signed and took the gear back to his room. He sat on the bed thinking about the tactics for tomorrow night but soon gave up. He would have to respond to the situation as it unfolded.

The following morning James went to see the Colonel. It might be his last visit and he wanted to say goodbye. He had become quite fond of the man. And in any case he had a few other preparations to make.

'Good morning, Sergeant. How did you get on yesterday? Did you find the Tank?'

'Yes, Sir, the action is going to happen tonight and by tomorrow it will all be over one way or another.'

'Well, I wish you the best of luck. You've more bottle than I'll ever have, but be careful.'

'Can I use the phone, please?'

'Yes, go ahead.'

James picked up the phone and dialled Inspector Collins.

'Hello, Sir. Sergeant MacDonald here. Can you do me a favour and pull any patrols or roadblocks out of the Market Hill area? Only I'll be working in that area tonight and I don't want to bump into any of your men. That way no one will get hurt.'

'That's not a problem. I'll have that sorted by tonight. Can you tell me what's going on or is it hush-hush?'

'No, I can tell you. I've found out who the mole is. It's an ex-SAS soldier who has gone over to the other side and tonight is the end of the road for one of us.'

'Bloody hell! You do get involved in a big way. You find trouble wherever you go.'

'Story of my life, Inspector. Story of my life.'

There was a bit more banter and then James went on to make a similar call to Major Randall. As he put down the phone a second time, James let out a sigh. Well, that was that. He had cooked his goose. Everything was ready. He looked up at the Colonel.

'I think I've covered everything. I'll leave you in peace now, Sir.'

'Well, good luck, son, and you come back – and that's an order! If you don't, I'll have you court-martialled.'

'I'll do my best, Dad!'

James left the office laughing and went back to his room. He cleaned his weapon, fitted the night sight, then wrapped stripes of hessian around it, making sure it didn't block the sights. When he was happy with it, he put it on the bed. Next he went to his ammo box and took out the knives and just one of the Walthers and one spare mag. He sharpened the knives and put them on the bed ready to strap on. He cleaned the Walther and the two mags. In the box he saw Stony's watch that Jill had given him and he put it in his pocket for luck.

Time was getting on. He put cam cream on to his face and the backs of his hands, strapped on the knives and filled his water bottle. The Walther went in the right-hand trouser pocket, spare mag in his left; he put on the cape and helmet, and picked up the SA8. He was ready to go. He jumped up and down to check that nothing rattled; it was all right. He went to the MT shed and on the way across the yard he felt as if he were being watched by a hundred pairs of eyes. The jungle drums had been beating again. The Colonel had promised him a ride in the Land-Rover and there it was waiting for him, the engine already purring. It was all done with the minimum fuss, as if he were taking part in a normal patrol. As they drove away, he loaded his weapon and put the safety catch on.

They dropped him at the track that led to the water tower. James disappeared into the wood and cut some of the undergrowth and fitted it into the camouflage netting on his helmet and cape. When he was happy he moved into the killing zone, moving like a shadow. The moon cast deep shadows so that every tree seemed to hide something menacing.

James knew that the best plan would be to find somewhere to hide and let the Tank come to him, but if they both had the same idea they would be there for ever, so he decided to keep on the move, all the while stopping, looking and listening, all the while making sure that he didn't stand on any dried twigs that would give him away. The hairs on the back of his neck were standing up on end, telling him he was getting close, even though there were no other signs, no tracks and none of the undergrowth had been flattened. It was just a feeling he had, call it intuition.

He stopped, got close to the ground and crawled forward, stopping and looking though the night sight. Still nothing. The moon was getting higher in the sky and the shadows were shorter than they had been an hour ago. He lay still and had an idea. He would try to draw The Tank's fire. He took

Stony's watch out of his pocket and tied it to a twig in the undergrowth. Next he tied a length of vine to the twig so that when he pulled it the watch would dance and catch the moonlight. He lay down and took up a fire position and looked through the night sight. He pulled the vine and the watch started moving. Then he saw a slight movement and then a burst of gunfire. Shit, the bullet had grazed his left upper arm! He took aim and fired off a couple of bursts. He heard a yell. He knew he had hit The Tank but where and how badly he was wounded he would have to find out. That could be dodgy.

James moved forward but not in a straight line. He skirted around and came in from the side. As he got close, he could hear moaning. The Tank was trying to take the pain. He peered through the undergrowth. A bullet had smashed through his teeth and lodged in the jawbone; the other one had hit his cheek and ripped half the ear away.

He was trying to speak to James and it took a while for him to understand what he was saying.

'James, you've the title … You're the best … Please finish it.'

Without hesitation James pulled out the Walther and fired two rounds into his old comrade's head. It was all over.

James went to the gate of the wood yard and found the envelope and put it in his combat jacket pocket. He felt the blood running down his arm and it was hurting like hell. He got out his field dressing and tied it around the arm to stop the bleeding. It was stinging like mad but he knew it was a flesh wound and no bones had been hit. Just another scar to add to his collection.

There was a phone box outside The Ulsterman's Arms. He rang Inspector Collins.

'Hello, Sir, can you do me a favour?'

'Are you all right?'

'I'm hurt but I'll live. Can you pick up a body from the

wood yard and give me a lift out of here. I'll meet you at the wood yard gates. Is that all right?'

'Sure, give me fifteen minutes and I'll be there.'

'Thanks.'

James sat down by the wood yard gates and waited. He pulled out his water bottle and had a good swig. He was feeling sorry for himself – he had just killed a man who had once meant everything to him. He heard the engines of the Land-Rovers before he saw them.

Inspector Collins got out and walked over to James.

'You sure you're all right. You don't look too good. Let's get this body and then we'll get you sorted. We'll take you to the nearest hospital.'

James took the Inspector to where the body lay and while they were putting The Tank into the body bag James went and found the watch. Remarkably, it was still working, although the bracelet was buggered. He looked at it and silently thanked Stony.

Chapter 15

When James woke up his arm was giving him a lot of pain and his mind was running over the previous night's events. He was feeling a little bit sorry for himself, then he remembered the envelope in his combat jacket pocket. He opened it and started to read.

Hello, son.
If you are reading this then you've taken the title and you'll probably be known as the man who stopped The Tank. Congratulations.

As promised the man you're after is Brian Reece, a member of the Oireachtas – the Irish parliament.

Tank Sherman.

James wiped a tear from his eye and put the note back in the envelope. He decided to go and see the Medical Officer before he went to see the CO and report what he had found out.

He put on his uniform and his one-armed combat jacket and walked over to the medical centre. He waited his turn with two other soldiers.

When he went into the surgery, Captain Hudson barely looked up.

'What can I do for you, Sergeant?'

'Could you've a look at my arm, please, and give me something for the pain?'

'Well, let's have a look and see what you've done.'

'I didn't do it! It was someone else who shot me.'

'Funny!'

He was a miserable sod, not even a smile; no sense of humour at all.

The MO undid the bandage and pulled it away from the wound. He was a bit heavy-handed; paying him back for cracking a joke, no doubt. James just grimaced and took the pain. He wasn't going to give Captain Hudson the pleasure of hearing him shout.

'When was this treated?'

'Late last night, soon after it happened.'

'Well, it's clean enough. You were very lucky, Sergeant. Fifty millimetres to the right and you could have lost the arm.'

'No, I was *unlucky*, Sir. Fifty millimetres to the left and it would have missed completely.'

Captain Hudson put some antiseptic cream on the wound and re-bandaged it. He went to a cabinet and took out packet of paracetamol. He gave them to James.

'Take two tablets every four hours but do not exceed the dose, Sergeant, and I'll have another look in a couple of days.'

'Thank you, Sir. Will do.'

Next stop, the cabin. The section were cleaning their weapons ready for the patrol that night. As James walked in you could have heard a pin drop – everyone had stopped talking and looked at him.

'Hello, lads, everyone all right?'

'Yes, Sergeant,' they all answered together.

Then Doughy piped up. 'How did you get on last night? We saw you leaving. It was very impressive but why don't we use that sort of camouflage? … And Sir, we would have come with you, if you had asked.'

'That's three questions in one, Doughy. The first one: I'm still around so it must have gone all right. The second one: you will be using that equipment but for the patrols we're doing at the moment it wouldn't help a lot – just imagine walking down the high street with grass and undergrowth sticking out of your helmet and cape. The last question, I appreciate that you all would be there if I'd asked, but I fight by my own rules and it had to be a fair fight – me against him. Has that answered your questions?'

'Yes, Sergeant, but we still would have liked to have helped.'

'Your time will come. Don't rush into it.'

'At least you've been honest with us.'

'Corporal Brown, I see we've got the Keady area to patrol tonight. Is that correct?'

'Yes, Sergeant.'

'Well, you remember a little while ago we touched on roadblocks; well, tonight if you work out the route so that we're on the road from Keady to Castleblayney, this side of the border, we'll meet a UDR roadblock and then you'll see how it works. We want to be there between 2400 hours and 0030 hours. Is that all right.'

'Yes, Sergeant, will do. Do you want me to bring the route to you when I've worked it out?'

'No, Corporal, it's your patrol and I trust you to sort it out.'

'Thank you.'

'See you later, lads. I'm going to see if they will give me a new combat jacket or they might put me on a charge for damaging government property.'

They were all laughing as he walked out of the cabin. As he left he heard Tiny saying to Corporal Brown:

'Corporal, that's one hell of a soldier and we've been lucky to have him with us. It's the way he makes the right decisions and acts straight away, I would be pleased to be half the soldier that he is!'

James went to his room, removed the night sight from his SA80 and folded the camouflage cape and went over to see the Colour Sergeant.

'Hello, Colour, items returned: one night sight, one

camouflage cape and Hessian. Can I have a new combat jacket, please?'

'I'll sign these back in first but I don't know about the jacket. That could cost you.'

'I just told my lads that if they worked hard they could get promoted to Colour Sergeant and be the richest man in the barracks.'

'You've got to be joking! Who would want a buy a combat jacket with only one sleeve?'

'A one-armed man but I don't think there's many of them about.'

'Not in the Army anyway.'

James signed for the combat jacket and returned to his room and started cleaning his weapon and was nearly finished when the orderly knocked on the door.

'Come in.'

'Sergeant, Colonel Wiseman would like to see you in his office. Did you know I spend more time coming to fetch you than anyone else in the barracks?'

'That's the trouble with being popular, though it keeps you fit, Corporal. Thank you.'

'Fit be buggered! More like knackered.'

James walked over to the office and knocked on the door.

'Take a seat, Sergeant. I've just had Major Tompsett on the phone and he said that there'll be a helicopter here to pick you up on Friday at 1900 hours and you are to report to him Monday morning at 0900 hours and you are to take all your equipment with you.'

'I'm surprised they want me back. I must have done something wrong – that's the only time they've ever wanted me back. Still I'll find out Monday.'

'But at least they're giving you the weekend off, so it can't be all bad, can it?'

'No, I should be able to spend the weekend with my girlfriend. That will be good.'

184

'Do you think you'll be back again?'

'One never knows, Sir, but the longer I'm away the younger you're going to look. I'll see you later. I really need to get my head down ready for tonight.'

'You out tonight?'

'Yes, Sir, on patrol with the section.'

At 2100 hours the section formed up inside the gates. Corporal Brown was in the lead, James was at two and then the rest of the section; Doughy was the tail-end Charlie. The guard opened the gates and they were on their way along the main road. Just as they left the town, tied to two trees was a white banner with red writing:

BRITS GO HOME!

Paint had been allowed to drip down from the letters to make it look like blood.

'The bastards.' cried Lambie. 'Let's pull it down and get rid of it.'

'Leave it! Don't anyone touch it. Use your fucking brains. Ask yourselves two questions. One, why is it at a height that you can't reach without climbing: because they want you to pull it down. Two, why wasn't it put up in town? Answer: because of the damage that would be done to property and there's always a chance that a bystander could be hurt ... Corporal, all round defence, then come with me and let's have a look.'

Corporal Brown gave the order, then he and James went to have a look. They reached the trunk of the first tree; the only thing there was the main strings holding the banner to the tree. They moved to the second tree, and there it was: an IED taped to the trunk. Anyone pulling the banner down would pull out the pin and then boom – whoever had pulled it down and any others in the way would be blown to bits.

James went over to and checked the IED to see if there was any anti-handling device fitted. Lucky enough there was

185

none, so James held the pin in and cut the string with one of the knives that he had strapped to his leg. He then cut through the tape holding the bomb to the trunk, leaving the tape attached to the bomb. Next he wrapped the tape around the pin to keep it in place, cut the banner down and folded it up and they went back to the section who by now were moving again. James dropped back beside Lambie.

'Yours, I believe.' He handed the banner to him. 'If you had pulled it down you would have been the lamb in the shepherd's pie.'

'I'm sorry, Sergeant. I didn't think but it won't happen again. I've learnt my lesson and you saved my life. Thanks!'

'I only did it because I don't want to write to your mother.'

He went back to his position, chuckling to himself.

'Corporal, double time for a while. I want to make up the time we lost dealing with that banner.'

They made up the time in three separate stints and the patrol was soon approaching the UDR roadblock from the south. They were about two hundred and fifty metres from the roadblock when the silence of the night was shattered by gunfire coming from that direction. A car had crashed through the block and was speeding towards them and heading for the border.

'Scatter and if they get past me wait until they have passed, then take them out.'

James ran thirty metres towards the car, then he took aim and fired a burst, then another and then a third. The first burst hit the driver, the second took out the two rear passengers, the third was sprayed across the full width of the car. The driver lost control and hit the bank and the car shot up into the air and landed on its roof in a shower of sparks as it slid along the road. It came to an abrupt stop when it left the road and landed in the hedge.

'Corporal, take some men and check the car out. Be careful! They may still be alive.'

'Yes, Sergeant.'

'The way he shoots I'll bet anyone a tenner that they're all as dead as dodos.' Lance Corporal Minter remarked.

'Tiny, radio in contact and wait out, and then move up to the roadblock with me.'

'Yes, Sergeant.'

James started running to the roadblock. As he approached he was shouting, 'Army, Army, Army.' He saw a UDR man.

'I'm Sergeant MacDonald. Who's in charge here and can I help?'

'Sergeant Giles is in charge. We've one officer down and that's all I know.'

James found the sergeant kneeling over the figure lying in the road.

'Sergeant Giles, I'm Sergeant MacDonald. What have we got here? Can I help?'

'I'm glad you came along when you did, Sergeant. She's been shot in the shoulder and I can't stop the bleeding. I'm not very good at first aid.'

'What's her name?'

'Corporal Fay Conner.' James went down on his knees, leant over her, took hold of her hand and felt her pulse.

'Hello, Fay. You stay with me now. My name is James. Will you keep talking to me?'

'Yes, but I just want to sleep.'

'No, talk to me! Are you married and have you got any children?'

'No I'm not married and I don't have any children, but I would like to get married one day.'

'I'm sure you will. Have you got a boyfriend? He's a very lucky guy if you have.'

'Not at the moment.'

'Sergeant, bring the Land-Rover over and let's have the headlights on full beam, so I can see what I'm doing.'

'Are you *the* James?'

'What one?'

'The one who saved Kate when she was taken hostage?'

'Yes, why?'

'Please save me! I don't want to die not here in the road.'

'When will the ambulance be here? Have you got an ETA?'

'There have been three major incidents in Belfast and they can't give me any times. They reckon it could be an hour or one and a half, or not at all.'

'Tiny, radio in and tell them I want a ambulance out here as soon as possible. The MOS plus medics and I need an ETA.'

'Straight away, Sergeant.'

'Fay, you are not going to die. Trust me. I'm going to cut your clothing away from the wound and try to stop the bleeding.'

'Yes, James, but it hurts like mad.'

'I bet it does but I'm afraid I'm going to hurt you, but stay with me and just keep talking. I know what it's like. I took a bullet in the leg and it hurts like hell.'

James pulled the Velcro and opened the flap and pulled out one of his knives. He cut her clothing away from the wound and also cut the field dressing off that the Sergeant had put on; it wasn't stopping the flow of blood. The bullet was lodged against the shoulder blade but she was still losing a lot of blood. He grabbed his field dressing and his own first-aid kit and he took out a couple of Tampax.

'This is where I have to apply a lot of pressure. Are you ready?'

'Yes, James, I'm ready.'

'Good girl. You owe me a date when you're better, all right?'

James pushed the Tampax into the entry hole and wrapped the field dressing tight over the top.

'Tiny, give me your field dressing so I can immobilize the arm, then it will give her some relief.'

Tiny passed James his field dressing and he folded the dressing in half to find the centre. He then looped it around her neck and placed her arm across her chest. Next he wrapped the dressing around her wrist at a comfortable height and then tied the other end to her belt so she couldn't lift it up or push it down.

'Nearly finished, Fay. What are you going to buy me for dinner?'

'Anything you like. What do you fancy?'

'How about you for starters?'

'James, are you chatting me up?'

'Yes and why not? Have we got a date then?'

'It's a date then.'

'I'm the lucky one to have a date with the prettiest girl around these parts.'

'Sergeant, they have just come back. The ambulance will be here in fifteen minutes but the MO is not very happy. He's moaning and he said he's going to have words with you.'

'Good, maybe he will do his job and save lives. Fay, I'm going to give you a sip of water and a couple of painkillers, all right?'

'Please.'

James gave her a couple of the paracetamol tablets that the MO had given to him. She sipped the water.

'Sergeant.' It was Lambie.

'Yes, Corporal.'

'They're all dead, Sergeant. You've done it again. They didn't know who they were up against.'

'Good, they didn't make the border. Find out what the UDR do with the bodies and get it sorted will you?'

'Yes, Sergeant.'

'Fay, how long have you known Kate?'

'About three years and all she does is talk about you ever since you brought her back.'

'All good I hope.'

'Oh yes.'

'Let' have a look and see if we've managed to stop the bleeding. Is that all right?'

'Be gentle! I don't want to go through that pain again.'

'It won't hurt you anymore. Trust me.'

James didn't take the field dressing off but just checked that there was no blood seeping through it or the side of the dressing; it seemed to be holding.

'There I told you I wouldn't hurt you anymore. I think the Tampax has done the job.'

'You used a Tampax?'

'Yes, think about it. It copes with the blood you lose during your monthly cycle so why shouldn't it work on a bullet wound? In days long ago the wounds from swords, spears and battle axes were horrendous, so the doctors carried cobwebs to do the same job.'

Tiny appeared. 'Sergeant, I've just been on the radio to get the RUC to pick up the bodies. Inspector Collins will be out here in about fifteen minutes' time.'

'Well done, Tiny. Thanks. Fay, do you like dancing and would you like to go again?'

'Yes I used to go dancing and I would like to go again. Are you offering to take me?'

'Yes, why not? But you've to stay with me and fight this all the way. Will you do that?'

'Yes and I want to see Kate's face when she finds out that I've met you and have a date.'

'Well, there you go.'

'James, I'm cold.'

'Not as cold as Kate was the first time I met her. She was blue.'

'She told me what happened.'

James stood up and undid his webbing and laid it alongside the SA80 on the ground. He took off his combat jacket and laid it over her.

'There now, you've had the same treatment that Kate had. Is that better? Are you feeling warmer?'

'Yes, but you lay beside her and held her in your arms.'

'Yes, but that was in a bed not in the middle of a road in the middle of nowhere.'

Tiny came running over.

'The ambulance is here with the QRF, Sergeant.'

'Well, get the ambulance as close as you can and ask Sergeant Giles which is the nearest hospital and tell the medics.'

'Yes, Sergeant.'

The medics came over with a stretcher and the MO had a saline drip in his hand. The medics gently lifted her on to the stretcher and the MO gave James his combat jacket back while the medics covered her in blankets. The MO fitted the drip into Fay's hand and the medic asked Tiny to hold the drip and the two medics carried Fay to the ambulance. Captain Hudson turned to James.

'I'll see you in the medical centre tomorrow because I've got to get her to hospital.'

'Yes, Sir.'

The MO walked over and got into the back of the ambulance and they drove off following the QRF.

'Sergeant Giles, I'm sorry but since I arrived here I seemed to have taken over and it's your show. I brought the section along so they could see how a roadblock was set up and how it operated.'

'I'm glad you came along when you did. You probably saved Corporal Fay Conner's life and you stopped them getting away across the border. They were probably the ones who caused the carnage in Belfast and that's why they ran the roadblock. I'm sorry they didn't get the chance to see the roadblock operating.'

'Do you know what happened in Belfast?'

'All that came over on the radio was that there were three

bombs in different locations. I don't know how many casualties but that's why there was no ambulance for the Corporal.'

'Don't you work with the Army and the RUC and help each other with equipment and ambulances, or even do joint operations. Surely that would ease the pressure?'

'No, but to be honest you wouldn't want to borrow our equipment. Most of it is worn out in any case. Even the Land-Rovers we have to bump-start because the batteries are knackered.'

'Will you get Colonel Kelly to give me a ring tomorrow and I'll see what I can do to help you. Maybe things could get better. I'll speak to Colonel Wiseman.'

'The RUC are here. Thank you for your help; it was much appreciated.'

'You're welcome and take care.'

James shook his hand and they got into the Land-Rovers. The one they'd used to illuminate Fay wouldn't start and had to be pushed to get the engine to start. Inspector Collins came over.

'Fucking hell, I might have guessed it was you again, but I thought you would be resting that arm of yours?'

'That's all right and you'll be pleased to know that I've been called back to Hereford, so you'll be made redundant. I fly out Friday night at 1900 hours.'

'It's a wonder your CO wants you back because you are more trouble than you're worth.'

'Come off it, we've made you look good with all the arms and munitions you've collected. By the way have you raided Four Oaks Farm?'

'Yes, both the haystacks were false. We emptied both and we had to make two journeys and our friend Mr Dermot McNally is in custody right now. He tried to deny everything, but we have him nailed and he won't worm his way out of this.'

'Now you can see what I mean.'

'All right, you win. I can't get one over on you, can I?'

'Not really but keep trying. I enjoy the competition; it keeps me on my toes.'

'I've got another raid tomorrow for a Major Randall. Do you know who he is?'

'Yes, Major Randall is in charge of 14 Intelligent Unit out of Loughgall. It's a mobile phone shop in Portadown owned by a Michael Finn.'

'Yes, how do you know?'

'That's where I followed The Tank to. He was living in the flat over the shop. It could be a bomb-making factory.'

'Anyway I shall miss you when you're gone. They say you always miss a pain in the arse. So what have you got for me here? Another scene of carnage and destruction I can see.'

Chapter 16

James woke up screaming. He was wet through with sweat. He had had a nightmare and he had seen the faces of the men he had killed, especially the ones he had killed up close. It was like looking at a police line-up, but now there was an extra face to haunt him and that was The Tank and he was the worst of all because it was like killing his own father. He knew The Tank would haunt him for the rest of his life. He got out of bed and picked up his washing kit and walked down to the ablutions block. He had a strip wash so he didn't get the bandage on his arm too wet. After that he felt a lot better and he went back to his room and got dressed in his uniform and made his way across the yard and into the mess.

'Hello, Cookie.'

'Hello, Sergeant, would you like your usual full English?'

'Yes please, that will do nicely.'

'I hear that you'll be leaving Friday. Is that right?'

'Yes and I bet you'll miss me.'

'Yes, the boys will have nothing to talk about. Did you know you're the only man to carry Tampax in his webbing?'

'It worked and I also carry Durex. Did you know they hold a gallon of water and if you put them on the muzzle of your weapon it will keep the rain out and in desert conditions it keeps the sand out of the barrel. But there's always a better use.'

'I wonder what that would be.'

'Use your imagination, Cookie.'

'I am, Sergeant, but I bet you a tenner that the jungle

194

drums will be quiet all next week. Have you seen the papers this morning? It's all in there about the bombs in Belfast.'

'No, I came straight over here.'

'Well, if you get your coffee I'll find it and bring it over to the table with your breakfast.'

'Thanks, Cookie.'

Cookie came over with his breakfast and a newspaper tucked under his arm. He placed the food in front of James and sat down opposite him to show him the headlines: 'Twenty-nine dead as bombs rock Belfast.' James scanned the article; it was the end paragraph that interested him the most. It stated that the local constabulary believed that the four bombers had been shot dead at a UDR roadblock as they tried to break through to get across the border in the early hours of this morning; also that one UDR officer had been shot and wounded, though her condition was understood to be stable.

'May I borrow this paper, please?'

'You can have it, Sergeant. I heard it was you who stopped them getting away. You stood in front of the car and took them all out. Is that true and they didn't stand a chance?'

'What would you expect me to do – thumb a lift?'

'No, but you wouldn't get me within five miles of a situation like that. I'll take my chance with a frying pan.'

'If I come back again I'll take you for a ride and show you the Mountains of Mourne.'

'I would sooner see the Blackpool Tower.'

Cookie stood up and returned to the kitchen area while James finished his breakfast. On the way out he waved the paper.

'Thanks for this, Cookie. I'll see you later.'

'You're welcome.'

James walked out and made his way to the Medical Centre to see the MO. James waited for his turn to go in. He was called in and he stood to attention and saluted.

'You wanted to see me this morning, Sir?'

'Yes, Sergeant, what do you think you were doing last night?'

'I was trying to save the life of a UDR officer by getting an MO and ambulance as quickly as I possibly could.'

'We don't go out for outsiders; we're for military use.'

'Do you think I would have got the radio operator to radio in with a request for the ambulance if I could have got a civilian ambulance quicker? I know you despise people like me for what we do, but we're a lot like you.'

'How do you work that out, Sergeant?'

'You find that someone has a cancer, you operate and take it out, but sometimes it comes back again. When I find a cancer and I operate, they never come back again. If you read this and you'll see why we do the job.'

James handed him the paper. The MO adjusted his glasses and read the article.

'Now you can see why I requested the ambulance? And you tell me, Sir, that a UDR officer is not military. Anyway I leave on Friday so you won't have to worry about me. May I go, Sir?'

'Let's have a look at that arm.'

'No need to bother, Sir; it will heal on its own and I don't want to waste your time.'

James stood to attention, saluted and walked out of the door, picking up the paper on his way. Once he got outside he took a deep breath and then walked over to the Colonel's office.

The orderly looked up. 'The old man said that when you came in he would like to see you.'

Inside the Colonel looked harassed.

'Take a seat, Sergeant. I hear you had a busy night last night. What happened between you and the MO? He said that you ordered him out with the ambulance.'

'I *requested* the MO to come out. Because of the explosions in Belfast, the UDR couldn't get an ambulance and they had

196

an Officer down and the nearest one was here. If he hadn't come out I would have requested a chopper from Bessbrook.'

'That puts a different light on the situation.'

'Too bloody right, Sir. I wish you were with me last night just to see what happened because you are the one man who could make a big difference and alter things.'

'How can I make a difference?'

'Well, it's only a suggestion but if you got together with Colonel Kelly, Major Randall and Inspector Collins, you could work out a strategy on how to share resources *and* information. It could help all of us. Last night was a prime example ...'

They discussed the issue at length. James felt passionate about the subject and the Colonel, although he thought it was a good idea, raised possible objections.

'Well, I tell you what ...' the Colonel began.

The red phone rang, cutting the Colonel off in mid-sentence. He picked up the phone and talked for a while. James quickly guessed it was Colonel Kelly. Would he have any news?

The Colonel replaced the receiver and looked at James.

'You never told me all that happened last night. Colonel Kelly is really impressed this time. You've got quite a fan club.'

'Did he say how Corporal Fay Conner is. Is she all right?'

'Yes, she's fine. She has had the bullet removed and will make a full recovery. She's a very lucky young lady.'

'It's better to be born lucky than rich, Sir.'

'True, but where were we? Ah, yes we were talking about cooperation with the others. Well, if you go and get yourself a coffee, I'll speak to Major Franklin and I'll get him in with yourself to draw up a list of how we can cooperate. Then I'll call a meeting. How's that?'

'Brilliant, Sir.'

197

'It looks like your stay here is going to have some long-term results, Sergeant. You've taught us a lot.'

James was in the mess.

'Hello, Sergeant, what would you like? We've some nice steaks today. Real monsters, probably horse meat, but I've had no complaints up to now.'

'Go on then, you've twisted my arm, but can you tell me what part of the horse it is?'

'No but it's not Shergar. He has been missing too long. Would you like mash and roasties, or chips.'

'I'll have mash *and* roast potatoes, peas, carrots and gravy, please.'

'Coming up! Is that right, you're leaving tomorrow and not on Friday as expected?'

'It's news to me. I've not heard anything but knowing how things seem to get around it could be true. Why don't you start your own newspaper and call it *Cookie's Gazette?*'

'Do you think I could make money at it? I could be the editor … No, I've changed my mind, I only have a six-month tour of duty and I wouldn't get my money back on the printing machines I would have to buy,'

'So you're going to stick with the jungle drums then?'

'That would be the best way forward. No libel suits. I can always say it was only what I heard.'

'You're a crafty bastard. Not like that horse. You're always one jump ahead of the rest.'

'Got to be, Sergeant.'

When James had finished his dinner, he walked over to Cookie, who was standing behind the counter with his hands on his hips.

'You've not come to complain, have you?'

'No, that was very, very nice, but I have to gallop over to see the Colonel now.'

'What again?'

'Yes again! I'm an important fellow.'

Cookie was laughing as James left the mess and walked over to the Colonel's office.

'Hello again, Sergeant, take a seat. I hope you've a couple of hours to spare. I'm going to miss our little meetings, though I feel a bit like your secretary with all the messages I've taken for you this morning.'

'You're not as good-looking as some secretaries I know, Sir.'

A grin came over the Colonel's face.

'I wouldn't want to sit on *your* knee either.'

'I can understand that, Sir.'

'Major Tompsett has been on the phone. There is a chopper coming in on Thursday night instead of Friday; it will be here at 1900 hours.'

'I knew that, Sir; it was on the jungle drums.'

'Jungle drums? What do you mean?'

'Well, if you want to know what's going on around here just ask the cooks; they're sure to know.'

'Is that how it works?'

'Yes, Sir.'

'Also Major Randall has been on. The raid on the mobile phone shop in Portadown has been a complete success. They found bombs in the process of being made and they have taken a load of papers away. They still have to go through them but Major Randall reckons they should get a lot more information from them once they take a good look at them.'

'It's good to get a result, Sir; I'm very pleased.'

'It's a great result, Sergeant. Well done! He also said that Michael Finn is blaming your old friend The Tank because he has gone missing and they don't know where he is. And he had only just heard about the raid on Four Oaks Farm.'

'Well, let them believe that's what happened because it will give us time to get some more intelligence from the papers and they will be a bit wary of Mr Brian Reece and the men that he recruits as informers.'

'And one more thing. Major Randall reckons the Irishman you asked about, the one who smokes those Dutch cigars called Meharis is a Morgan Finlay, but at this point in time they don't know if he's in Northern Ireland or in London. As soon as the Major finds out he will let you know. He also said well done and that it's been a pleasure working with you; he hopes he gets the chance to work together again.'

'That's nice of him, Sir, but we're only halfway there on our cigar-smoking villain.'

'Why do you want him so bad, Sergeant?'

'Because he was the one in charge of the IRA cell that ambushed Stony, Sir.'

The Colonel looked at James and he could see the hate in those ice-blue eyes, just like the ice water that ran through his veins. He was glad that he could call him a friend because he would hate to have him as an enemy.

'I would hate to be in his shoes when you catch up with him.'

'The trouble is when will that be?'

'Let's change the subject; I can see steam coming out of your ears. Have you seen the final draft that was drawn up with Major Franklin about cooperation?'

'No I know what's in it but I was at dinner while the Major was having it typed up.'

'Well, here is a copy. It's fantastic and will give us a good start, although it's a pity that you won't be here to see it implemented.'

'True ...' James hesitated for a moment. 'If I may, Sir, I would like to recommend that Corporal Brown gets his third stripe, but if he gets it I don't want him to know it was me who recommended him.'

'To be honest, you've beaten me to it. I was going to ask you if you thought he was ready for his third stripe. Now I know.'

'He's a very good soldier, Sir; he learns fast and deserves the chance to shine out without me being there to hold his hand. He will do his best for the men and I know you'll be very proud of him.'

'Well, that's settled. We'll promote him tomorrow at 1600 hours and I would like you to attend the parade.'

'I'll be there, Sir. May I ask one more favour before I leave tomorrow night?'

'Yes, Sergeant.'

'May I borrow the car?'

'What do you need the car for?'

'Well I promised Corporal Fay Conner that when she was better I would take her out dancing and now I've been pulled out, I can't keep that promise, so I would like to go and see her and explain the situation.'

'You're an old softie at heart. Yes, I'll sort it out. What time would you like it to be ready?'

'Zero nine thirty hours, Sir, then I'll have plenty of time to be back for your presentation at 1600 hours. But don't tell the lads what an old softie I am otherwise it will be broadcast on the jungle drums all around the barracks.'

'I think that's it for now, Sergeant. I'll see you tomorrow.'

'Thank you, Sir.'

James stood to attention, saluted and left the office. He went to his room and packed his belongings, but left out the casual clothes he needed for the hospital. He locked his ammo box and pushed it back under the bed; he was all ready for a hectic day tomorrow.

At 0930 the following morning James was on his way to the hospital to see Fay, keeping a watchful eye on his rear-view mirrors. Passing by the hospital's perimeter fence, he noticed a big sign fixed to the fence with wire:

GUARD DOGS OPERATING

James smiled to himself and thought, Bloody hell, I'm glad that they're not operating on me! Then as he walked towards the main entrance he was in stitches. There was another notice:

FAMILY PLANNING
USE THE REAR ENTRANCE

James was still smiling as he walked into the main entrance. He bought a box of milk chocolates and a bunch of red and yellow roses from the hospital shop and then went over to reception.

'Good morning, Sir, can I help you?'

The girl was a slim blonde with a fresh complexion and a broad Irish accent.

'Yes, could you tell me in which ward I could find Miss Fay Conner, please?'

'Just one moment, Sir … Ah there she is, it's a separate room. Number 101. It's on the first floor. Have you been in before?'

'No, could you tell me where it is, please?'

'If you go through those doors behind you and then go up the stairs to the first floor, then turn left and go along the corridor as far as you can. Next turn right and its halfway down on the right-hand side; the doors have got the numbers on them.'

'Thank you, could you tell me what time the next bus is?'

'Where to, Sir?'

'Room 101; it sounds miles away.'

The girl started laughing and she looked at James admiringly.

'You're young and fit; you'll make it. And if you don't you're in the right place to receive treatment.'

She was still laughing as James disappeared through the doors to the stairs. He climbed up to the first floor and walked along the corridors and found room 101. He knocked on the door and walked in holding the flowers in front of his face.

'Who are you?'

'I'm the one.'

'What one?'

'The one who saved Kate.'

He pulled the flowers away and then she recognized him.

'James, it's nice to see you. I wasn't expecting you to visit me in hospital.'

'You're looking a lot better than the last time I saw you. I didn't realize how beautiful you are. How are you feeling?'

'I still have a lot of pain but it's still early days yet. It will take time to heal but I'm on the mend. Anyhow give me a kiss because I want to say thank you.'

'Why thank me? You've not got the flowers or the chocolates yet and they might not be for you.'

'No you silly idiot – for saving my life.'

'I'm getting quite a collection of saved women but you did as much as I did; you are a fighter.'

James put the flowers and chocolates on the bedside cabinet and bent over the bed and kissed her gently on the lips, lingering a little. Just at that moment a doctor walked in the room.

'What's going on here then?'

'Nothing yet. You came in too early, you spoilsport.'

'Miss Conner, is this the Tampax man?'

'Yes, this is James.'

'Pleased to meet you! We had a laugh when we saw what you had plugged the wound with, though it worked well. If you hadn't stopped the bleeding, she wouldn't be here now.'

'Did you take the bullet out of her?'

'Yes, it was lodged against the shoulder blade but she was very lucky; it hadn't damaged the bone. Anyway it's been nice to meet you, Sergeant. I'll call in later, Miss Conner.'

'Thank you,' she said. 'Now where were we?'

James bent over and kissed her again.

'I believe that's where we were.'

'Yes, I remember now.'

'No brain damage then. On a more serious note, Fay, I came in to see you today because I've been called back to the UK and I fly out tonight so, unless they send me back, I'll not be able to take you out for that dance. I don't like breaking a promise!'

'Do you think you'll come back?'

'You're a soldier like me and we go wherever they send us and who knows where it will be.'

'But if you do come back, will you give me a call. I'll give you my number.'

Fay folded up the piece of paper and passed it to James who put it in his back pocket of his jeans.

'You see I've put it next to my heart.'

'Is that where your heart is?'

'No my wallet.'

'Please come back!'

There was a tear in her eye and her voice was trembling. James put his arms around her and held her really gently, being careful not to hurt the wounded shoulder.

'Come on, babe, remember whatever will be will be. I believe I've heard that somewhere before.'

'You silly sod, it's the words of a song.'

'I hate clever dicks and intelligent woman.'

'But I'm not an intelligent woman, so why are you being nasty to me?'

'Because if I was nice to you, you would start doing the girl thing, crying, and I don't want a wet shoulder. Anyway I have to get back – I have to be on parade this afternoon – but I want you to keep smiling and get better as soon as you can.'

'I'll be all right, James, and I'll look forward to your call.'

James gave her a kiss and left.

*   *   *

At 1600 hours James took up his position alongside Corporal Brown. Colonel Wiseman came out of the office followed by Major Franklin, The Regimental Sergeant Major called the parade to attention, marched over to the Colonel, stood to attention and saluted.

'Parade ready for inspection, Sir.'

'Thank you, Sergeant Major.'

The Colonel walked up and down the ranks, stopping every so often to talk to individual soldiers. Once he had finished he stood in front of the parade and the RSM gave the order.

'Stand at ease!' followed by 'Stand easy!'

The Colonel addressed the parade:

'Gentlemen, if I call your name I want you to come and report to me: Corporal Brown.'

Corporal Brown came to attention and marched out and halted at attention in front of the Colonel. He saluted.

'Corporal Brown reporting, Sir.'

'Corporal Brown, I'm pleased to say you've been promoted to Sergeant and well done, you deserve it.'

The Colonel handed him his three strips to sew on to his uniform.

'Thank you, Sir.'

He stood to attention and saluted then returned to his position in front of the section.

'Lance Corporal Minter.' Lance Corporal came to attention and did exactly the same as his Corporal had done.

'Lance Corporal Minter, you've been promoted to full Corporal. You've a very high standard to keep up but I know you can do it, so good luck.'

'Thank you, Sir.'

He stood to attention, saluted and marched back to his position at the rear of the section.

'Private Baker.'

Private Baker stood to attention and marched out and did the same as the other two.

'Private Baker, you've been promoted to Lance Corporal and good luck to you.'

'Thank you, Sir.'

He stood to attention, saluted and marched back to his position in the ranks.

'Sergeant MacDonald.'

James jumped to attention and marched towards Colonel Wiseman. What the hell did he want him for? He stood to attention in front of the Colonel and saluted.

'Sergeant MacDonald reporting, Sir.'

'Sergeant MacDonald, as you are leaving tonight I would like you to have this shield with the regimental badge on it as a token of our respect for you as a soldier; you've proved that you are one of the best.'

'Thank you, Sir, I feel very proud to have this honour.'

'Before you go back to your position I would also like to give you these crowns. You are now promoted to Sergeant Major.'

'I'm sorry I'll have to decline. My colonel would never allow me to take it, Sir.'

'*Your* colonel had no choice but to accept it, you were recommended by Colonel Kelly, Inspector Collins, Major Franklin, Major Randall and myself, and he was told in a forcible way that if he didn't agree we would take the matter higher.'

'Well, it's nice of you to go to so much trouble so how can I refuse and not accept it. Thank you, Sir.'

'When you're dismissed, will you join me in the office for a drink? Though you know it will have to be a coffee because of the rules.'

'I would be pleased to join you, Sir.'

'Good because I've another surprise for you.'

'Thank you, Sir.'

James saluted, did an about-turn and returned to his position in front of the section.

There were two more promotions for soldiers from another section and then the RSM took over control of the parade.

'Parade, Parade, Shun.'

Everyone on parade stood to attention.

'Officer on parade. Parade dismiss!'

When James entered the Colonel's office, he had the surprise of his life. Sitting in the office with the Colonel was Colonel Kelly, Inspector Collins and Major Randall.

'I told you I had another surprise for you. These gentlemen wanted to congratulate you and say thank you for all the hard work you have done for them.'

Inspector Collins was the first one to stand up and shake James by the hand.

'Good luck, Sergeant Major. You'll be missed and as you say I'll be redundant now.'

'Thank you, Sir. You're a crafty lot. There are no motors in the yard to give away your presence.'

'No, they're all in the MT shed out of the way.'

Colonel Kelly grabbed James by the hand.

'Well done, you're one hell of a soldier. Things are going to be very quiet around here when you've gone. It's going to take weeks before every topic of conversation among the Green Finches isn't about you.'

'I saw Corporal Conner today, Sir, and she's doing well and should be back with you soon.'

'I've heard all about it. She told me how she was looking forward to that dance.'

'Well, I promised, Sir, and I don't like breaking a promise so I had to give her the reason why.'

Colonel Wiseman looked at James. 'We've had our first

meeting about your ideas and everyone is in agreement that it's exactly what's needed. We're going ahead with the whole package that you and Major Franklin worked out.'

James beamed. 'I'm pleased to have worked with all of you and maybe one day I'll be back. I'd like to thank you all for your cooperation. I'm afraid I'll have to go now, Sir, because the helicopter will be here in thirty minutes.'

James shook their hands again and went to pack his final few possessions. Taking a last look around to make sure that nothing was left behind, he put his helmet on, picked up the shield and beret and made his way to the MT shed where a lorry was parked outside. James jumped in the back and put the shield and beret in one of the cases that had already been stowed away. As the lorry drove away he took one last look at the barracks and felt a pang of sorrow. He would miss this place! Well, that was a turn-up for the books!

Later that night he parked his car in the parking bay at the rear of Candy's flat. He got out his case and locked the car and found the spare key to the flat. He climbed the stairs and unlocked the door to the flat and walked in. He went through to the living room; the flat was in darkness. He heard a noise coming from the bedroom. He opened the door. Candy was in bed with a young man in his early twenties.

'What the hell is going on?'

'You didn't ring to let me know you were coming.'

'I didn't think I had to! Anyhow I wanted to give you a surprise and I've certainly done that.'

'Go into the living room, James. I'll be there in a minute.'

James went into the living room and put the light on. Candy came out of the bedroom, doing up her dressing gown.

'Well, you've not answered my question.'

'I was going to tell you as soon as I saw you.'

'Well, tell me now.'

'I thought I could do it but …'

Just then the young man came out of the bedroom, looking at James and then at Candy.

'Is everything all right, Candy?' he said.

James gave him his answer.

'No, fuck off back to the bedroom out of the way. We need to talk about a few things.'

He took one look at James and saw the hate in his eyes and got out of the room as quickly as he could.

'Well?'

'As I was saying I thought I could be on my own but I was getting lonely and needed someone that would be here for me.'

'I told you how it would have to be. I said that I wouldn't be able to let you know when I would be back or where I was.'

'I know and I really believed I would be able to manage but I couldn't … I was going to tell you.'

'So that makes everything all right. You told me you loved me and you wanted to be with me.'

She got up and went to the bedroom and came back with the engagement ring that James had bought her and handed it to him. He took it and put it in his pocket. He placed her key on the coffee table.

'Just look after yourself, Candy. I don't think *he* will be the one you settle down with; he ran like a bleeding rabbit but maybe he makes love like one too.'

He kissed her on the cheek and picked up his case.

'Goodbye.'

'I'm sorry. Goodbye, James.'

There was a tear in her eye.

As James climbed into his car he wondered where the hell he would spend the weekend. He wasn't quite ready for the barracks.

Chapter 17

'Hello, Jill. It's James.'

'Hello, James. It's good to hear your voice.'

'I only just got back last night and it's the first opportunity I've had to ring you. How have you been keeping?'

'To be honest, not too well. I've been suffering from depression, though some days are better than others.'

'Have you been to the doctor's?'

'Yes, he said that it was only to be expected after the ordeal that I've been through. He prescribed some tablets and that was it. He said that if I didn't feel any better in three weeks I should go back and see him again.'

'You'll have to give the tablets time to work. Did you manage to get the headstone done?'

'Yes, it was installed the end of last week. It's very nice; you'll have to come down and see it.'

'Well, I have a few days off. I'll come down on Friday and spend a couple of days in Kent, I'll book into a hotel.'

'There is no need to, James. Since Ben's dad died he spends most of his time with his granddad, so you can have his room. What time will you be here?'

'Somewhere around six.'

'I'll do us something to eat; it will be nice to catch up on old times again.'

'Is there anything you want me to bring?'

'No, just yourself.'

'Take care, Jill, and I'll see you on Friday.'

'See you, James. Bye.'

*   *   *

On Friday afternoon Jill opened the door and greeted him with a kiss on the cheek. He gave her a bunch of flowers.

'Are these for me? They're beautiful, come in and I'll put these in water. I've a nice vase that my dad gave me.'

James went and sat on the settee while Jill went and found the vase and arranged the flowers.

'You look well, James,' she said as she returned with the vase. 'I'll not ask where you've been. I know the score there.'

'You look amazing! What have you been doing since the last time I saw you?'

'Not a lot to be honest, only looking after Ben, but like I said he spends more time with his granddad these days. I have a part-time job at Tesco's. It's only stacking shelves but I can work flexi-hours so I'm always here when Ben gets home … I'm forgetting my manners, would you like a glass of wine?'

'I would love one.'

Jill fetched a bottle of cool white wine and poured out two glasses.

'Excuse me, James. I've just got to finish the dinner. If you like, take your wine through to the dining room. I'll not be too long.'

James had been in the dining room for about ten minutes when Jill came in from the kitchen with two dinners, a large one for James and a smaller one for herself. It was a proper roast dinner. Jill handed James the gravy boat.

'Thank you! This looks wonderful. You must have spent ages in the kitchen and if it tastes as good as it looks it will be out of this world.'

'It's just nice to have someone to cook for. With just me and Ben, you tend to make do.'

After the meal James helped take the dishes out to the kitchen and put them in the sink and then turned to Jill.

'What would you like to do tonight?'

211

'I hadn't thought about it, to be honest.'

'How about if we take a walk down to The White Horse; it's only just down the road.'

'That would be nice. I would enjoy doing something different; I've not been out at all.'

'Well, you go and get ready and I'll be mother and do the dishes.'

'Thanks.'

She went upstairs and changed and James washed up and dried the dishes. When she came down she looked like a film star though her eyes were sad. She went and got her coat off the hook.

'James, are you ready?'

'Yes, coming.'

Jill locked the door, grabbed hold of his arm and they slowly walked down the road. It was dry but there was a little bit of a nip in the air. The sky was free of cloud and the moon was a full circle and you could see the stars.

The White Horse was a big old country pub, with whitewashed walls and dark oak beams. They could hear music as they approached: there was a live band playing the old favourites. They walked in and went to a table. He took her coat and hung it on the back of her chair.

When James returned to the table with the drinks, Jill was talking to a large woman in her forties. She was overweight with chubby rosy red cheeks as if she worked outdoors.

'James, this is Mrs Hill. She and her husband own Old Crooked Farm about a mile and half up the road from me.'

'Call me, Rita, please.'

'Pleased to meet you, Rita.'

He shook her hand.

'This is James,' Jill went on. 'He was a very good friend of Roy's and he has come down to see the headstone I got.'

'You'll be pleased. I've seen it and it's very impressive. Must have cost her an arm and a leg.'

'I'm looking forward to seeing it.'

'What do you do for a living, James?'

'I'm in the Army.'

'Not *another* soldier, Jill.'

'What's wrong with soldiers?' replied Jill.

The woman looked embarrassed. 'Nothing at all ... You know. Look, I'd better find my old man. He might think I've run away ... He wishes! See you later!'

James raised his eyebrows.

'Oh she's all right, a bit of an old gossip but her heart is in the right place and she would do anything for you.'

'Your reputation has just gone up in smoke. You'll be known as the scarlet woman.'

Soon after a man in his thirties came over, quite good-looking, one of those who fancies himself but can't get around to it.

'Hello, Jill, I've been meaning to come around to see you. We've not seen you out and about for ages.'

'No this is the first time I've been out in ages.'

'May I give you a call? We could go out to dinner sometime. I would like that.'

I bet you would! James thought. She's the best catch around here but even with all your dosh she's far too good for you. You're only after one thing.

'I don't think so, but thank you,' Jill said firmly.

'Go on! You don't know what you're missing.'

James stood up and whispered in his ear. 'The lady said no and if you don't push off you'll find out what you are missing.'

The man glared at James. 'See you around, Jill.'

And off he went back to his mates at the bar, probably bragging about how she was going to go out with him to dinner in the near future.

'What did you say to him, James?'

'I just said the lady said no and did he know what no meant.'

'Thank you, James. He can be a bit of a pest, especially when he's been drinking.'

'Forget him! How about a dance and I'll show you just how rusty I am. I've not danced in ages.'

'I think we'll manage all right.'

James put out his hand and she took hold of it and he led her to the dance floor. He put his arm around her and pulled her close to him. She laid her head on his shoulder. He could smell her perfume; it was deep and musky. Her hair was brushing his cheek, his arm was around her waist and he could feel her breasts pushing against him. He was either in heaven or in hell.

Back at their table James excused himself and went to the toilet. He was just washing his hands when the yuppie walked in and spotted him. He was drunk and angry.

'She doesn't belong to you! I've a good mind to teach you a lesson and give you a good hiding.'

'I'm just looking out for her. Anyhow what lesson are you going to teach me? Are you a vicar.'

'I've met your sort before. You just poke your nose into other people's damn business.'

'And I've met *your* sort before. You think you're God's gift to women and you can't stand being rejected.'

'I'll show you.'

He took a swing at James, who neatly sidestepped and with a powerful right hook hit him in the solar plexus. The man dropped to his knees. He crawled to the toilet and was violently sick. James threw him a parting shot.

'I think I've taught *you* a lesson. Set your sights lower.'

On the way back to the table he stopped at the yuppie's table.

'I think you had better take your mate home. He's in the toilet. He can't take it.'

'Thank you, mate. We'll go and get him.'

'Well done, lads.'

James went back to Jill.

'Are you ready to go home?'

'Yes. I've had a wonderful time, but it's tiring.'

James stood up and walked around the table and helped her on with her coat. They walked out into the chill night air. As they crossed the car park the yuppie's mates were helping him into a big posh car.

'Do you think he has had too much to drink?' Jill said.

'Yes, some people just can't hold their drink.'

He put his arm around her and they walked up the road to the house.

'Which is my room?' he asked once they were inside.

'Top of the stairs, turn to the right and it's the door right in front of you. While you take your case up I'll make coffee.'

'Thank you. Be back down in a minute.'

James went upstairs and put his case in Ben's room. There was a single bed in the corner and posters of David Beckham and the Manchester United team all over the walls. He even had a United bedspread.

'You'd would never guess what football team Ben supports and who his idol is,' he commented as he sipped his coffee downstairs.

Jill sat down beside him.

'All he dreams of is going to see them live.'

'Maybe one day he will.'

'Do you want to watch a film? I can put one on.'

'Sure, that will be nice.'

'Would you like to pick one?'

'No, put on what you want.'

She went over and picked a film – Patrick Swayze and Jennifer Grey in *Dirty Dancing*. She came back to the settee and sat with her legs over the arm and her head on his lap. Almost without thinking he found himself stroking her hair and the side of her face.

After the film had finished they went upstairs. James kissed her goodnight and went into Ben's bedroom. He stripped down to his boxers and lay on the bed listening to the rain hitting the windows. All of a sudden there was a terrific clap of thunder and the lightning lit up the bedroom. A second later there was a scream.

James jumped out of bed and ran into Jill's bedroom. Jill was sitting up in bed naked with her head in her hands.

'Are you all right? What's the matter?'

'When it thundered I thought about the lorry that hit Roy's car. It must have sounded like that.'

'Don't think about it. Try to go to sleep.'

She looked at James and noticed the scar that he had that ran all the way across his belly.

'I know I shouldn't ask but how the hell did you get that scar?'

'I got too close to the sharp end of a knife. Now try to go to sleep and I'll go back to bed.'

'Please stay with me, James.'

He looked at her and their eyes met.

'Are you sure?' he asked. 'Is it right?'

'I don't care! Please, I just want to feel your body against mine and to feel loved once again.'

'I don't know. It doesn't seem right.'

'Don't you fancy me then? Please, James, don't make me beg for it because I will.'

James got into bed and held her close and kissed her tenderly on the lips. But it was like she had been given an electric shock and she had gone berserk. She put her foot in the top of his boxer shorts and pushed them down with her foot and before they had come off she had rolled on top and was guiding him inside her. She gave out a squeal and then started moving up and down, increasing speed. Her breasts were fairly small and the dark nipples were hard and pointing at him. Then all of a sudden they exploded together, then she lay still.

'O my God, it seems like ages since I had an orgasm like that; it blew my mind away. Thank you.'

'It wasn't bad, was it?'

'James, you know it was fantastic, or would you rather have gone for a run over the Beacons?'

'Not really. You did all the work; I didn't even break into a sweat.'

She cuddled into James and put her head on his chest. Soon they fell into a deep contented sleep.

The next morning after breakfast they got in the car and drove down to the cemetery. They walked over to the grave. The headstone was in the shape of a cross, with two photographs fitted in frames and inlayed into each arm of the cross. In the centre was carved the Winged Dagger, the cap badge of the SAS Regiment. Down the main body of the cross was the inscription:

In loving memory of Roy Burke and his daughter Nikki Burke.
Gone but not forgotten.

James stood there with a tear in his eye, holding Jill and still looking at the headstone.

'You've done them proud and it's fantastic.'

'Well, Stony, old buddy,' James said to himself, 'all I can say is that the debt is paid in full with interest.'

Jill had the interest last night.

Glossary

DSC	Distinguished Service Cross
ETA	Estimated Time of Arrival
GPMG	General Purpose Machine Gun
HMTD	Explosive
IED	Improvised Explosive Device
IRA	Irish Republican Army
MM	Military Medal
QRF	Quick Reaction Force
RUC	Royal Ulster Constabulary
SA80	Semi Automatic Rifle
SLR	Self-loading Rifle
UDA	Ulster Defence Association
UDR	Ulster Defence Regiment
UVF	Ulster Volunteer Force
Uzi	Machine Pistol